Hope isn't hard to find. . . .

Gin-Yung squeezed Todd's fingers. "Elizabeth is a wonderful person, Todd. Don't throw away what you have because you feel some sort of obligation to me."

"Believe me, I don't feel obligated," Todd insisted. Even though he had felt that way before, Todd was now truly speaking from his heart. "I want to be here. Right now *you're* the most important person in my life. And I'm here for you. I'm not going anywhere."

Gin-Yung's eyes misted over. "I'm so glad." She exhaled with relief. The incessant beeps of the heart monitor permeated the intensity of the moment. Gin-Yung gave Todd an exhausted smile. "We should start the game," she said lightly.

Todd balanced the miniature Scrabble board on her legs. "You go first."

Staring intently at her rack of tiles, Gin-Yung shuffled them around a bit. "You've given me some great letters." She picked up four tiles and placed them carefully on the board.

They spelled *hope*.

Bantam Books in the Sweet Valley University series.
Ask your bookseller for the books you have missed.

#1 COLLEGE GIRLS
#2 LOVE, LIES, AND JESSICA WAKEFIELD
#3 WHAT YOUR PARENTS DON'T KNOW . . .
#4 ANYTHING FOR LOVE
#5 A MARRIED WOMAN
#6 THE LOVE OF HER LIFE
#7 GOOD-BYE TO LOVE
#8 HOME FOR CHRISTMAS
#9 SORORITY SCANDAL
#10 NO MEANS NO
#11 TAKE BACK THE NIGHT
#12 COLLEGE CRUISE
#13 SS HEARTBREAK
#14 SHIPBOARD WEDDING
#15 BEHIND CLOSED DOORS
#16 THE OTHER WOMAN

#17 DEADLY ATTRACTION
#18 BILLIE'S SECRET
#19 BROKEN PROMISES, SHATTERED DREAMS
#20 HERE COMES THE BRIDE
#21 FOR THE LOVE OF RYAN
#22 ELIZABETH'S SUMMER LOVE
#23 SWEET KISS OF SUMMER
#24 HIS SECRET PAST
#25 BUSTED!
#26 THE TRIAL OF JESSICA WAKEFIELD
#27 ELIZABETH AND TODD FOREVER
#28 ELIZABETH'S HEARTBREAK
#29 ONE LAST KISS

And don't miss these Sweet Valley
University Thriller Editions:

#1 WANTED FOR MURDER
#2 HE'S WATCHING YOU
#3 KISS OF THE VAMPIRE
#4 THE HOUSE OF DEATH
#5 RUNNING FOR HER LIFE
#6 THE ROOMMATE
#7 WHAT WINSTON SAW

Visit the Official Sweet Valley Web Site on the Internet at:

http://www.sweetvalley.com

SWEET VALLEY UNIVERSITY®

One Last Kiss

Written by
Laurie John

Created by
FRANCINE PASCAL

BANTAM BOOKS
NEW YORK · TORONTO · LONDON · SYDNEY · AUCKLAND

RL 6, age 12 and up

ONE LAST KISS
A Bantam Book / April 1997

Sweet Valley High® *and Sweet Valley University*®
are registered trademarks of Francine Pascal.
Conceived by Francine Pascal.
Produced by Daniel Weiss Associates, Inc.
33 West 17th Street
New York, NY 10011.

ISBN: 0-553-57053-6

Published simultaneously in the United States and Canada

Bantam Books are published by Bantam Books, a division of Bantam
Doubleday Dell Publishing Group, Inc. Its trademark, consisting of the
words "Bantam Books" and the portrayal of a rooster, is Registered in
U.S. Patent and Trademark Office and in other countries. Marca
Registrada. Bantam Books, 1540 Broadway, New York, New York 10036.

PRINTED IN THE UNITED STATES OF AMERICA

OPM   0 9 8 7 6 5 4 3 2 1

To Lisa Nathan

Chapter One

"How much time does she have left, Dr. Madison?"

Even after Todd Wilkins choked out the question, he could hardly believe he was asking it. He searched around the drab hospital waiting room, hoping to find reassurance that nothing was really wrong, that he had taken everything the wrong way. But there was no hope to be found—not in Dr. Madison's bleak stare, not in the damp tears on Elizabeth Wakefield's eyelashes.

This is not real. This is not happening. Todd repeated the words over and over again in his mind like a mantra. He squeezed his fists in staunch determination when he silently declared, *No. Gin-Yung Suh is not dying.*

His thoughts were interrupted by the sound of strangled cries rising up from the corner of

1

the hospital waiting room, where Gin-Yung's older sister, Kim-Mi, was comforting their grief-stricken mother on the couch. Todd turned away from them, instead focusing his dry, stinging brown eyes on the doctor's blindingly white lab coat. He struggled to block out the family's wrenching sobs, but it seemed impossible.

"We're looking at days," Dr. Madison murmured grimly as she ran a brisk hand through her short auburn hair. "But with something like a brain tumor, there's no real way of knowing. If Gin-Yung suddenly takes a bad turn, it could be a matter of hours."

Todd shook his head in disbelief. "Um . . . excuse us a minute, Doctor," he mumbled before he pulled Elizabeth over toward the water fountain at the far end of the waiting room.

"What is it?" Elizabeth asked urgently.

Todd stared deeply into his girlfriend's sad blue-green eyes and wiped away a tear that was rolling down her cheek. "You know, Liz," he muttered deeply, "I just can't believe it."

"I know. Neither can I."

"No—you don't understand what I'm saying," Todd blurted, waving his hands in front of him. "I mean, I *don't* believe it. I don't think it's true." The words spilled out of his mouth quickly, clumsily, as if they were beyond Todd's control.

2

"Gin-Yung can't be dying. It's not possible."

Elizabeth's eyes widened in horror. "Todd, what are you saying?"

"I mean, maybe it's just some weird virus she caught in London," Todd argued, placing his hands firmly on Elizabeth's shoulders. "Maybe she's just exhausted from her trip—a bad case of jet lag or something. You know how doctors can overreact sometimes. How do we know this woman isn't jumping to conclusions?"

"The family has known about Gin-Yung's brain tumor for quite some time. Kim told us herself," Elizabeth replied, her voice wavering.

Todd shook his head furiously, ignoring the violent wave of nausea that was ripping through his stomach. "I just . . . I just don't know," he said anxiously. "It all seems so hard to believe."

He hoped that Elizabeth would agree with him, but she simply dug a tissue out of her bag and wiped her nose. Todd looked away from his girlfriend and stared across the room at Gin-Yung's sister and mother, who were huddled together on the couch and heaving with sobs. *It just can't be true,* Todd told himself. *How could Gin-Yung hide such a terrible secret? Why would she keep it from me?*

Elizabeth reached for Todd's hand and laced her slender fingers with his. Strands of golden blond hair had loosened from her ponytail and were clinging to her tear-dampened face. "I know this is a big shock for you . . . for all of us. But it's not a mistake, Todd. Gin-Yung has a terminal brain tumor."

"How do you know?" Todd cried. "You haven't even seen her! How do you know?"

Elizabeth brought her cool, soft hand up to Todd's face and stroked his cheek as if she was trying to calm him down. "No doctor in the world could make a mistake like that. Gin-Yung is dying, Todd. She's really dying."

The gravity in Elizabeth's voice resonated deeply through Todd's heart and mind. Her words reached down into a painful place where Todd was keeping his true feelings tightly locked away. For a brief instant he took a deep breath and opened himself up, almost willing to accept what he knew had to be true. But a surge of agonizing emotion rose up, forcing Todd to quickly squelch his belief and lock it away again.

"I can't . . . I just can't believe it," he whispered, holding on tightly to Elizabeth's hand. He felt as if he were sliding over the edge of a cliff and that she was the only one who could save him. "I think I need to see for myself." Todd ran his fingers through his wavy, light brown hair and exhaled loudly.

Elizabeth half smiled up at him and nodded quietly.

4

"Would it bother you if I went to see her?" Todd watched Elizabeth's lovely, delicate face carefully, hoping she wouldn't protest.

"Of course not," she assured him, shaking her head emphatically. "You *should* go see her. She was your girlfriend, after all."

She was your girlfriend. The words echoed in Todd's mind. To him, it felt as if it had been years since he and Gin-Yung had dated. In the few months that Gin-Yung had been in London for her sports journalism internship, the two of them slowly began to drift apart. They didn't keep in touch nearly as much as Todd had thought they would, and their telephone conversations were strained and awkward. He blamed it on the distance, figuring that when Gin-Yung returned to campus, they'd continue where they left off.

What Todd *didn't* count on was Elizabeth Wakefield coming back into his life.

Elizabeth had been Todd's girlfriend all through high school, but things fell apart when they first arrived at Sweet Valley University. As the star rookie of the Sweet Valley University basketball team, Todd quickly developed an out-of-control ego. He got anything and everything he wanted, except for one thing: He couldn't get Elizabeth to go along with taking their relationship to a more physical level. He broke up with her almost immediately—and he'd regretted it ever since.

Todd went on to date a few women who were on the wild side before he finally settled down with Gin-Yung, a feisty but down-to-earth sports reporter. And Elizabeth was happily dating Tom Watts, a journalist with whom she worked at the WSVU television station.

Todd knew he'd been a jerk to her, but during the time he and Elizabeth had been apart, he'd changed. And when Gin-Yung went abroad and Elizabeth and Tom broke up, suddenly Todd found that he had a chance to win his first love back. As much as he cared for Gin-Yung, Todd felt deep in his heart that Elizabeth was the person he was meant to be with forever.

Now Elizabeth was his again. But between Gin-Yung's unexpected return to Sweet Valley and the news of her illness, Todd couldn't escape the feeling that everything he had wished for—and got—was on the verge of crumbling.

With a long, cleansing sigh Todd leaned forward and pressed his forehead against Elizabeth's. "Are you sure you don't mind?" he asked as he stared lovingly into her troubled eyes.

Elizabeth took both his hands in hers and let her long lashes drop toward her cheeks. "We can't think of ourselves right now, Todd. We have to do whatever's best for Gin-Yung."

You are so amazing, Elizabeth, Todd thought as he turned his head and pressed his cheek to hers, breathing in the warm, honey scent of her hair. A loving surge broke through the sorrow that had been surrounding his heart. He longed to tell her, *You really are too good for me. How did I ever get so lucky as to have a second chance with you?* But with Gin-Yung's mother and sister sobbing just a few yards away, he knew it was neither the right time nor the right place.

With Elizabeth's hand in his, he walked back to where Dr. Madison was standing. "Excuse me—I'd like to see Gin-Yung, if that's possible."

The doctor glanced down at her clipboard and flipped through a few pages. "She's in ICU room number six. But I have to warn you—" She paused for a moment, her mouth drawn into a tight line. "Gin-Yung's in a great deal of pain. We've done everything we can to make her comfortable, but the medication usually makes patients drowsy and listless. I just want you to be prepared."

"Paging Dr. Madison. Dr. Madison, please report to ICU room number four immediately," buzzed a voice through the waiting room speakers. Without another word the doctor turned around and headed down the sterile white hospital corridor.

A sudden tightness seized Todd's chest. *Be prepared?* he wondered anxiously. *Be prepared for* what?

"Todd?" A delicate touch on Todd's arm snapped him out of his trance. "Are you all right?" Elizabeth's eyes were wide with concern.

"Come on. Let's go," Todd commanded, knowing that if he waited a moment longer, he would lose his nerve. He began leading Elizabeth toward the hall that led to the intensive care unit. When he passed Kim and Mrs. Suh, he didn't look at or speak to them, afraid that if he did, his heart would split wide open.

Suddenly Elizabeth halted in her tracks. "I shouldn't go," she said firmly. "You need to be alone with her."

"But I need you. I . . . I don't think I can do this alone," he admitted plaintively.

"Yes, you can. Think about how awkward it would be for Gin-Yung to see us together," Elizabeth argued. "Even though she's given us her blessing, she's in a delicate state. Seeing the two of us together . . . who knows, that might upset her."

"I guess you're right," Todd answered wearily, letting go of her hand. He felt as if all rational thoughts had been drained from his head and replaced with a gigantic wad of cotton. The concept of what should and shouldn't be done so as not to upset someone in fragile health seemed completely foreign to him. It was something he'd never had to think about before.

"I'm going back to the dorm. Call me when you get home." Elizabeth stood on her toes and planted a sad, sweet kiss on the tip of Todd's nose. "I'll talk to you later."

Todd responded with a mournful nod and watched as Elizabeth headed toward the elevator. His entire body felt heavy, leaden, and weighted down. With arms dangling helplessly at his sides, Todd stood there, immobile, wondering what awaited him in ICU room number six.

Elizabeth barely made it to the edge of the hospital parking lot before she broke down in sobs. She wandered blindly past hazy rows of cars, gasping for air, aimlessly searching for the Jeep she shared with her twin sister, Jessica. Her heart ached from the impact of seeing the Suhs' crushed faces.

No one deserves to endure such a tragedy, she thought with a shuddering sigh. *Especially not someone as good and kind as Gin-Yung*.

Through a blur of tears Elizabeth miraculously found her Jeep, a bright red blotch at the end of the second row. She fumbled inside her purse for the keys and unlocked the door. *I wonder how Todd's doing*, she wondered as she slid into the driver's seat and slammed the door shut. *What is he going to see when he gets to Gin-Yung's room? Did I do the right thing by leaving him alone?*

After opening the glove compartment with trembling fingers, Elizabeth reached in and found a pack of tissues. Being both Todd's "old" and "new" girlfriend suddenly made her wonder where exactly she stood in all this. *It's not as if I can pick up some etiquette guide off the library shelf that will tell me what to do*, Elizabeth thought, wiping her eyes. She could picture the chapter heading: "How to Behave If Your Boyfriend's Ex-girlfriend Is Dying of a Terminal Illness." As Elizabeth grew older, she was beginning to see that what made life so hard was that there were no pat answers— you just had to stumble around in the dark and hope you ended up making the right decisions.

Elizabeth caught a glimpse of her red, swollen eyes in the rearview mirror and winced. "What *are* the right decisions anyway?" she asked her reflection. "Have I made any of them in the last few days?" As soon as the last question escaped her lips a pang of guilt tugged mercilessly at her. She knew it was far too soon to start speculating about how Gin-Yung's illness was going to impact her own life, but she couldn't help it.

Elizabeth groaned loudly and rested her arms and head on the steering wheel, her cheeks burning with shame. *Gin-Yung's dying, and all you can think about is yourself,* her conscience taunted.

"But what am I supposed to do?" Elizabeth cried out loud. "I *know* I should probably stay out of the way and let Todd take care of Gin-Yung. But what is that going to mean for *us?*"

Never mind that, her conscience whispered in response. *It's the right thing to do.*

A heavy sob rose from Elizabeth's chest and caught in her throat. "Right for who?" she choked out, her voice cracking. Letting go of Todd certainly wasn't the right thing for Elizabeth as far as she was concerned. It had taken a long time for them to be reunited—and their romance was even sweeter than it had been in high school. Aside from Jessica, Todd knew Elizabeth better than anyone else. They had a history together. Todd was her first love, the one Elizabeth always saved a place for in her heart even after they'd broken up. It had been Todd from the beginning, and Elizabeth believed—now more than ever—that it would be Todd in the end.

Tears poured down Elizabeth's face as she

squeezed her eyes shut in a vain effort to block out the harsh yellow sunlight pouring through the windshield. She wanted more than anything to be hard-hearted and selfish, to have icy blood running through her veins as she turned unflinchingly to Gin-Yung and said, without even batting an eye, "Todd's mine. I won't share him!"

If only Elizabeth didn't think about anyone but herself, didn't weigh the pros and cons before making even the smallest decision, didn't feel things as deeply and sensitively as she did. If only she didn't care.

But she did.

We can't think of ourselves right now, Todd. We have to do whatever's best for Gin-Yung. Elizabeth's words echoed in Todd's ears as he stood timidly in the middle of the hallway. What if the doctor *was* right? What if Gin-Yung was really dying? Todd sucked in a sharp breath, keeping a rise of panic at bay.

But he had to see her. He had to know the truth.

With a slow, reluctant turn Todd headed toward the long white corridor of the intensive care unit, moving one foot stiffly in front of the other. His head pounded in fierce, hammering blows. With cold, shaking fingers he kneaded the tension in his brow, his eyes fixed on the scrubbed white floor tiles. *What am I going to say to Gin-Yung when I see her?* he wondered. *What do you say to someone you know is dying?* Todd continued to stare at the floor ahead of him, not daring to look into the open doors of the other intensive care rooms he passed. The hall was ominously silent except for the squeak of Todd's basketball sneakers as he trudged apprehensively toward Gin-Yung's room.

When he reached ICU room number six, Todd turned his toes toward the door and walked in, eyes still grazing the floor. The room was dark except for a dim fluorescent light coming from somewhere on the far side. Todd stopped in the doorway, slowly lifting his gaze from the floor to the chrome wheels of the hospital bed, up to the orange blanket covering Gin-Yung's thin legs. Todd's frightened heart thundered as he watched the shallow rise and fall of Gin-Yung's chest. She was obviously having trouble breathing. Swallowing hard, Todd summoned his courage enough to move his eyes over until they finally came to rest on Gin-Yung's thin, sallow face. Her glossy blue-black hair was gone, replaced by a pale, grayish cap of stubble. Her sunken cheeks and closed eyes showed no trace of the healthy glow Gin-Yung used to have. She didn't look like the same person at all.

Todd looked up at the room number one more time, just to be sure. *Number six.* He fell against the door and reached for the knob to steady himself. The emotions he'd locked tightly away were screaming to get out. *It's true,* Todd thought, his lips quivering. *It really is true.*

"What are they doing to you?" he whispered, glaring at the tangled maze of tubes surrounding her. Skinny IV tubes were taped to Gin-Yung's right arm, feeding a clear liquid directly into her veins. A wider respirator tube was coming out of her mouth, while two smaller tubes pumped oxygen into her nose. Wires were taped to her head and chest, leading to the various monitors that beeped and hummed around her. And yet through all of this Gin-Yung lay completely still and silent, her dark, almond-shaped eyes closed.

I can't believe this is happening to you, Gin. It's so unfair. Tears suddenly sprang to Todd's eyes as he watched Gin-Yung breathe, the harsh light above the bed giving her skin a strange, otherworldly glow. He imagined himself lying there, surrounded by equipment, struggling to fill his own lungs with air, knowing he was going to die. A terrified sob wrenched out of his throat.

As if she heard him, Gin-Yung blinked slowly a few times, her eyelids opening a fraction. She

14

stared at Todd through half-closed eyes, blankly at first. After a few moments a tiny smile tugged around the thick white respirator tube.

Todd's fingers gripped the handle of the doorknob tightly. "Hi . . . Gin," he muttered, finding it hard to connect that name with the shadow of a person who lay there.

With frail fingers Gin-Yung pulled aside the respirator, her colorless lips curving into a weak smile. "Oh, Todd," she whispered hollowly. "Come closer . . . I can hardly see you."

Todd edged nearer, arms moving woodenly at his sides. A steady stream of salty tears trickled down his face as he stopped at the foot of the bed. He was afraid to get any closer to the delicate network of tubes and machines surrounding her, as if his very presence might cause them to break down.

But when Todd's sad eyes met hers, he recognized the faintest spark of the fire that had once burned so brightly there. "Oh, Gin-Yung . . ." Todd's voice broke as he gingerly placed his hand on her bony ankle. Even through the blanket it felt cold. "I don't know what to say—"

"You don't have to say anything," Gin-Yung interrupted in a raspy voice. Her red-rimmed eyes were damp.

Todd looked down. "Why did you keep this from me?"

"It's not that I didn't want you to know. . . ." She stopped to take a raspy breath. "I just couldn't find the strength to tell you."

"I could've helped you through this," Todd blurted almost mechanically, unsure if he really could have been of any help to Gin-Yung at all. But it seemed like the right thing to say at the moment.

"I know," Gin-Yung murmured, gently wiggling her foot against his hand. "But you're here now. That's what matters."

An awkward silence fell between them. What was Gin-Yung expecting from him? Was it more than he was willing to give? Todd wiped his face with his shirtsleeve, feeling burdened by the sudden responsibility and terrified that he was going to fail miserably.

"I'm so sorry, Gin-Yung," Todd choked, not knowing what else to say. "I'm just so *sorry*."

"Don't you dare make me cry, Todd Wilkins," Gin-Yung ordered, her thin voice wavering. "It hurts too much."

Chapter Two

"It's another beautiful Tuesday morning in southern California. Up next is the latest from Flies Without Wings. It's called 'Sanctimonium Superhighway.'"

"Jess! Turn that stupid thing off!" Elizabeth groaned, covering her startled ears with two throw pillows. She opened her swollen, tired eyes and looked at Jessica, who was dozing peacefully beneath her purple satin comforter despite the screeching rock music blaring from her clock radio. Her mouth was frozen in a maddeningly tranquil smile.

"Jess!" Elizabeth shouted, much louder this time, her temper shortened by the lack of sleep. *That's just one of the thousands of differences between me and my sister,* Elizabeth thought ruefully, still clutching the pillow to her head.

When something bothers me, I stay awake all night thinking about it, while Jessica can turn her brain off like a light switch. Occasionally Elizabeth envied that quality in her sister, but on this particular morning she found it completely infuriating.

"Wake up and turn off the stupid alarm!" Elizabeth hurled her pillow to the other side of the dorm room they shared, bopping her sleeping twin squarely on the head.

Jessica lay motionless, her face now covered by the thrown pillow. *Why should I be surprised?* Elizabeth thought. *After all, she's been known to sleep through earthquakes.* Anger trickled out of Elizabeth like air from a leaky tire, only to be replaced by a heavier feeling of remorse that settled in the center of her chest.

Elizabeth threw back her pink-and-white cotton bedcovers and removed the pillow she had thrown, afraid that if she didn't, Jessica would suffocate in her sleep. She snapped off the screaming alarm clock, watching in wonder as her sister began to stir gently.

"The dead has awakened," Elizabeth quipped.

"Good morning to you too, Miss Congeniality." Jessica stretched her arms overhead languidly as she woke with the dewy freshness of a newly hatched chick.

"Why didn't you turn off your alarm?" Elizabeth demanded wearily.

Jessica's long lashes fluttered open, her complexion pink and innocent. "*Someone's* grumpy this morning," she observed with a yawn.

"Can you blame me?" Elizabeth pounced on the edge of Jessica's bed, narrowly missing her sister's ankles by a few inches. "I hardly slept at all last night, and then, when I finally dozed off, your clock radio started blaring—"

"Look, I'm sorry I didn't hear the stupid alarm," Jessica interrupted. A slow, luxurious grin suddenly spread across her face as she rolled over onto her side. "I was too busy dreaming about Nick. We were shipwrecked on this gorgeous deserted island in the Pacific with nothing but coconuts, mangoes, and our love to keep us alive. I had the best tan *ever*, Liz," she said wistfully. "You should've seen it."

"No wonder you had so much trouble waking up," Elizabeth muttered.

Jessica's blue-green eyes glazed over as she began to recount the delicious details of her dream. "Luckily the boat we had been on was transporting a bunch of sports equipment. We had a Frisbee and a volleyball net and a croquet set. Nick even nailed a basketball hoop to a palm tree! And then we found a Jet Ski—"

An impatient frown twisted Elizabeth's lips.

"I'd love to hear more about your dream vacation with your boyfriend, Jess. But there's something really serious I need to tell you."

Her twin sister's playful smile faded and she immediately sat up in bed, obviously sensing that Elizabeth wasn't joking around. "What is it?" she whispered urgently, her features darkening. "Did you and Todd break it off again?"

Elizabeth hugged the pillow close and sighed. "It's not that. It's much worse than that. . . ." She trailed off, unable to describe the tragic scene she'd witnessed the day before in the hospital. Taking a deep breath, Elizabeth started again. "You know, of course, that Gin-Yung's back from England—"

"And now that she's back, Todd wants to start seeing her again," Jessica finished. Her left cheek dimpled angrily. "I *knew* Gin-Yung would sink her claws into him again as soon as she had the chance." She touched her sister's hand sympathetically. "Stop shaking your head, Liz. It's going to be all right. If Todd is going to double-cross you, then don't even waste your time thinking about him."

"Todd didn't dump me for her," Elizabeth blurted. "It's not about Todd—at least not directly."

Brushing a silky blond strand of hair out of her eyes, Jessica studied Elizabeth for a long moment, her brow furrowing. "What is it, then?"

"Gin-Yung's in the hospital." Elizabeth exhaled suddenly, unaware that she'd been holding her breath. Looking up, her eyes locked with Jessica's. "She has a brain tumor that can't be operated on. There's nothing the doctors can do." Elizabeth paused while a cold, ominous shiver trickled down her spine. "She's dying, Jess."

A look of paralyzing shock seemed to jolt Jessica to a state of full alertness. With bulging eyes and her jaw falling slightly open, she appeared to be having trouble comprehending the news. "She c-can't be," Jessica stammered, her fingers grasping the bedcovers tightly. "She can't be dying. I mean, she's—she's so *young!*"

Elizabeth toyed with a loose thread that was hanging from the hem of her long cotton nightgown. "I know. It just doesn't make any sense," she answered thickly. "I was with Todd at the hospital yesterday. The doctor told us that she doesn't have much time left."

Jessica reached out and gave her sister a supportive hug. "How's Todd taking all of this?"

"Not too well. It's a confusing time for him right now. When Gin-Yung left for her journalism internship, they were still together, and she was healthy. So much has happened since she's been away."

"The Thetas are going to freak when I tell them the news," Jessica said, chewing on a cuticle and staring off into space.

"*Please* don't tell your sorority sisters or *anyone,* for that matter," Elizabeth begged. "I don't think Gin-Yung wants anyone to know what she's going through."

"OK. I won't say anything," Jessica promised, sounding a little disappointed. She threw off her purple comforter and walked over to the tiny coffeemaker that sat on the edge of her desk. After rummaging around in the top drawer for a few seconds, she took out a packet of coffee grounds. "How did she look?" Jessica asked gently.

"I don't know. I didn't see her. But Todd has, I'm sure. He was going in to visit her when I left." Elizabeth felt a dull ache gnawing at her stomach, wondering how things had gone for him. Was everything better than it sounded—or worse?

Jessica turned around suddenly. "You mean you didn't go with him?"

"I thought he needed to be alone with her," Elizabeth answered defensively. *Maybe I did make the wrong decision,* she thought for a moment. *But Jessica doesn't understand the situation—besides, she handles things completely differently than I do.* Elizabeth jumped off the

22

bed and raised the blinds, turning her back so Jessica couldn't see the look of distress on her face. A yellow film of early morning sunlight spilled in through the window. "Todd and Gin-Yung have a lot to sort out by themselves. They didn't need me there."

Jessica raised an eyebrow. "I understand that, but you're forgetting that they used to go out," she countered, pouring the coffee into the filter basket.

"I haven't forgotten that at all," Elizabeth responded, staring quizzically at her twin. "What are you getting at anyway?"

"All I'm saying is that you and Todd just got back together, and now that Gin-Yung's in the hospital, what's going to happen?" Jessica reached for her short silk robe and put it on over her satin nightshirt. "I know you pride yourself on always doing the right thing, Liz. Aren't you going to feel *guilty* if you keep going out with Todd while Gin-Yung's in the hospital? And aren't you worried about what this whole thing might mean for the two of you?"

Elizabeth had been awake most of the night asking herself the same questions. As she was lying there, staring up at the shadows on the ceiling, Elizabeth came to the realization that she and Todd had their whole lives to be together. If they had to spend a few days, weeks, or even a few months apart so that Todd could comfort Gin-Yung in her final days, then it was worth the sacrifice. There was also the chance that things might come between Elizabeth and Todd in the meantime, but they had no choice but to take the risk. *Gin-Yung needs Todd right now, even more than you do,* Elizabeth had told herself. *It won't be forever.*

"Had to think about that one, didn't you?" Jessica prompted, snapping Elizabeth out of her reverie.

"Of course I've thought about it. And I'm terrified, Jess. I'm terrified that something might change between us." Elizabeth jammed her cold feet into a pair of fluffy pink slippers with determination. "But Gin-Yung is going through a horrible time. It would be best if Todd were there for her."

Joining her sister at the window, Jessica rested her hand on Elizabeth's shoulder. "So that's it? Gin-Yung's sick, so you're going to push all your feelings to the side?"

"How I feel isn't important," Elizabeth answered in a clear voice, trying to persuade Jessica just as much as she was trying to persuade herself. Her eyes misted over, frustrated by the difference between what her heart wanted and what she knew to be right.

"What?" Jessica rolled her eyes exasperatedly. "Stop playing the martyr, sis. I think Gin-Yung's got you beat in that department."

"Jessica!" Even though she knew her sister could get pretty callous sometimes, Elizabeth still couldn't believe her ears. "That's not fair at all. That's horrible!"

"Hey, I'm not saying I'm not sorry for Gin-Yung," Jessica amended. "But you can't ignore your own feelings here. You should fight for what you really want—no matter what the situation is."

"I can't do that." Elizabeth sighed, shaking her head sadly. "Not with Gin-Yung the way she is. It'll only make things worse."

"Jeez. You're acting like it's *your* fault the poor girl is dying," Jessica continued. "I mean, what if Todd spends all this time with Gin-Yung, and through some miracle she gets better? *Then* where will you be?"

Elizabeth's throat felt as if it were closing up. She could barely breathe. "Stop it!"

"Sorry." Jessica stroked her sister's head soothingly. "You're the one who's always telling me that rule number one for a healthy relationship is never to hide your feelings from the person you love."

Elizabeth turned toward Jessica. Her eyes were overflowing with tears. "You know something, Jess? Maybe there are a few exceptions to that rule."

As he stood in the doorway of his father's patent law office Tom Watts burned with rage. George Conroy was sitting at his desk, working, unaware of Tom's presence. Tom's smoldering eyes stared fiercely at the thinning brown hair of the man who'd taken away the part of Tom's life he'd held most dear. The evidence was right there, in the envelope Tom gripped tightly in his sweaty fist. *Let's hear you try to deny it now, George,* Tom thought bitterly as hot anger stung the back of his neck like a thousand searing flames. *I dare you.*

Mr. Conroy suddenly turned around as if he was pricked by the heat of his son's stare. A bright smile broke over his face. "Tom! Don't just stand there. Come on in!" His brown eyes sparkled as he motioned for Tom to enter his lavishly decorated law office. "I'm glad you were able to take some time out of your busy schedule to have lunch with your old man."

You make me absolutely sick, acting like there's nothing's wrong here. Tom's brown leather loafers burned a trail across the cranberry-colored carpet to his father's walnut desk, where he stood with arms folded boldly across his crisp white dress shirt.

"Have a seat," Mr. Conroy said, pointing to the ornately carved chair next to where Tom was standing.

Tom clenched his jaw. "No, I'll stand," he answered in a biting tone.

Concern flickered in Mr. Conroy's eyes, and his smile disappeared. "Is something wrong, Tom? Are you sick?"

"I've been wanting to ask you the same question," he spat back. Tom's tall, lean frame towered imposingly over the desk, the heat rising off his flushed face. *I accepted you so quickly,* Tom thought, clenching his hands into tight fists. *I even called you Dad. But trusting you may have been the biggest mistake of my life.*

It didn't matter anymore that Mr. Conroy was his long-lost biological father. It didn't matter anymore that Tom's yearning for the family he had lost in a tragic car crash had finally been fulfilled by Mr. Conroy and his children, Mary and Jake. As far as Tom was concerned, their relationship meant nothing now. Mr. Conroy wasn't a father, but a liar and a letch. He was a stranger who'd entered Tom's life for a brief and unfortunate time.

But that's going to change now, Tom seethed, his dark, blazing eyes sparking a confrontation. *At this moment I'm severing all ties between us, George.*

Mr. Conroy took off his gold wire-rimmed reading glasses and set them down gingerly on the desktop. Deep creases formed around his forehead and across his brow, as if he were aging before Tom's eyes. "What exactly is going on here, son?"

"Don't call me that!" Tom growled. "You have no right to call me your son!"

The color drained from Mr. Conroy's cheeks, his complexion taking on an ashen pallor. His troubled brown eyes fell on the envelope clenched in Tom's fist. "Am I supposed to just sit here and guess what's bothering you, or are you going to tell me?"

As if you don't know, Tom thought in disgust, not sure if he could stomach any more of his father's revolting lies. Mr. Conroy's blank stare only fueled the raging inferno in Tom's chest. What kind of person would repeatedly make passes at his son's girlfriend and then deny the whole thing? *A monster,* Tom answered silently. Only a monster would stand by and say nothing while his son's perfect romance crumbled, all because the son foolishly believed his father's word over his girlfriend's. And that was exactly what Mr. Conroy was—a monster.

"Why don't *you* tell *me?*" Tom threw the envelope across the desk. "The proof is right here."

With trembling fingers Mr. Conroy reached for the envelope. He cleared his throat, his pale lips drawn back tightly against his teeth, as if he already knew the contents without breaking the seal.

Hot blood pulsed rapidly through Tom's veins, but he took small comfort in his father's obvious distress. Underneath his blazing fury Tom felt as if he were dying inside. *How could George do this to me?* he wondered. *How could he do this to his own flesh and blood?*

"I—I can see why you'd be so upset," Mr. Conroy said, chuckling nervously as he loosened the knot on his imported silk tie. "But it's not what you think. If you'll let me explain—"

"There's *nothing* to explain!" Tom's sour stomach churned as he grabbed the envelope and tore it open. "Look at these pictures, George. *Look at them!*" Dozens of grainy, candid photographs spilled out across Mr. Conroy's desk—all of them of Elizabeth Wakefield. In one picture she was walking out of the library, her arms loaded down with books. In another she was in a bikini, sunbathing behind Dickenson Hall. There were pictures of Elizabeth getting out of her car, waiting in line at the cafeteria, standing in the window of her dorm room, walking to class. In every photo Elizabeth seemed completely unaware that she was being spied on.

Just looking at the pictures made Tom violently nauseous at the thought of his father shamelessly leering at sweet, unknowing Elizabeth through a telephoto lens. Kind, gentle Elizabeth, who'd never done anything to hurt Tom. Honest, innocent Elizabeth, who had been telling Tom the truth all along.

Mr. Conroy sat in heavy silence, his thin lips twitching. He slumped in his chair and turned his pale, pathetic face to the ceiling in what seemed to be a desperate attempt not to look at his son or at the images of Elizabeth that had been scattered all over his desk.

"Don't even try to deny it anymore, George," Tom warned, his voice shaking with outrage. "You *did* make a pass at Elizabeth Wakefield. Just say it."

Mr. Conroy remained eerily quiet. But suddenly his right arm jerked, knocking over his World's Greatest Father mug. He cried out in terror as hot coffee spilled over his desk. Gasping, Mr. Conroy snatched his monogrammed handkerchief from his pocket and frantically tried to mop up the coffee before it destroyed his precious photographs completely.

"What exactly do you think you're doing?" a frosty voice demanded.

Todd looked up in surprise. He had been all alone with a cup of bitter, watery coffee, hiding away in the safety and quiet of the sterile hospital cafeteria. But his brief moment of calm had just been broken by Gin-Yung's older sister, Kim-Mi, who was now striding purposefully across the dining area.

Todd tucked his rumpled rugby shirt into the waistband of his blue jeans and let out a deep, audible sigh. After he had watched Gin-Yung drift off into medicated sleep, Todd had found that he couldn't bring himself to leave the hospital. Whether it was out of a sense of duty or guilt, Todd couldn't be sure. But he didn't stay for long in Gin-Yung's room. Instead he tried to get some sleep on the hard, uninviting orange cushions of the waiting room couch. But all he got out of it was a stiff neck and a headache.

It had been an awfully long night. The last thing he needed was Kim getting on his case.

Kim jumped into the yellow plastic seat on the other side of Todd's table, her lips pinched into a scowl. She looked like she meant business.

"What exactly am I doing?" Todd parroted back as he opened a packet of sugar. "I'm having a cup of coffee."

Kim bared her teeth. "I mean about my sister."

Todd smoothed down his tousled hair and

held back a groan. "You used to be so nice, Kim. When did you suddenly decide that you had it in for me?"

"When you abandoned Gin-Yung," Kim shot back.

"I did *not* abandon her," Todd said, feeling his voice catch. "We grew apart when she was in London. It was a mutual thing."

A sneer curled Kim's lips. "That's a lie, and you know it." Her almond-shaped eyes challenged him. "You couldn't wait for Gin to leave so you could cheat on her. Whenever I talked to her on the phone, all I heard was Todd *this*, Todd *that*—meanwhile you and Elizabeth were dating behind her back."

Todd felt his blood pressure rising. *She has no right to talk to me like this,* he thought. *I came here to see Gin-Yung—not to be attacked.* He took a swig of coffee to fortify himself, but its bitterness only made him wince. "Listen, I never lied to her," Todd began. "When she came back to Sweet Valley, she knew that I was back with Elizabeth, and she was happy for us. Then she told me that *she'd* already been dating some other guy in London—some soccer player. So don't go condemning me for something your sister did too!"

Kim smacked her hands on the tabletop and nearly knocked over Todd's cup of coffee. Her voice shrilled through the dank cafeteria, arousing the attention of some people sitting nearby. "You are *so* naive, Todd! Or are you just feeling too guilty to see what's really going on here?"

Todd bit down hard on the inside of his lip. "What are you talking about?" he asked uneasily.

"Gin never dated anyone in London. She made that up because she knew how much you love Elizabeth. She wanted you to be happy, so she lied to you! And you were so desperate to go back to Elizabeth that you actually believed her!"

"But I really thought—" Todd's voice faltered. He leaned back and closed his weary eyes. *Kim's anger . . . Gin-Yung's illness . . . Elizabeth's love . . .* Everything swirled around and around in Todd's mind like a raging whirlpool, sucking him in deeper and deeper until he felt as if he were drowning in its vortex. Every time Todd thought he finally had his head above water, something came along to drag him down again. "Are you *sure* she wasn't dating anyone? Maybe she just didn't tell you."

Kim folded her arms across her chest defiantly. "Ask her yourself."

Todd sat in stunned silence, a sinking feeling in his solar plexus. *Gin-Yung* would *do something like that*, he realized. *She* would *want me to be with Elizabeth. After all, she's not going to live—* Todd cut off the morbid thought as a chill traveled swiftly up his spine.

No, it's not just that, he assured himself. *When Gin-Yung needed me the most, she was willing to let me go. As long as I was happy, she could be happy too.* Todd's eyes burned with suppressed tears. He could barely grasp what kind of strength and courage it must have taken for Gin-Yung to perform such a supreme act of unselfish love. Todd's heart swelled with a mixture of awestruck admiration and bittersweet tenderness.

But when he met Kim's cold, resentful eyes across the table, Todd grew suspicious. Was Kim really telling the truth, or was she just saying those things to make him feel even guiltier than he already did?

"Why are you still here, Todd?" Kim asked, her voice clad in frozen steel. "Why aren't you with Elizabeth? Is the guilt finally getting to you?"

Todd recoiled as if he'd been bitten by a snake. "I'm here because Gin-Yung needs me."

"Oh, really?" Her voice dripped with skepticism. "But do you *want* to be here? Come on, be honest with me."

Todd felt the oppressive weight of Kim's gaze bearing down on him. "Yes. I want to be here for her," he said stiffly. "I want to help Gin-Yung." What else could he say? He hardly knew what words were coming out of his mouth to begin with. He simply parted his lips and whatever Kim seemed to want to hear came tumbling out.

Leaning back in her chair, Kim's features softened slightly. "If you really want to be there for my sister, you'd better go all the way with it, Todd, or don't bother at all. I want Gin's last days to be as peaceful and happy as possible, and if you're going to mess around with her feelings, you can walk out that door right now."

A flash of outrage left Todd smarting. "How could you think I would be so cruel? Maybe I haven't handled things the way I should have, but I'm not some jerk who does whatever he feels like, not caring who gets hurt. I'm not like that."

"Good. Glad to hear it," Kim said evenly. "Here are the ground rules. You visit her regularly so she has something to look forward to. You show up when you say you will—not ten minutes late, not five minutes late—*on time*. I don't want Gin to waste *one minute* wondering where you are. You talk to her—not ten feet away, but right beside her. Don't be timid. Touch her, be affectionate. Do everything in your power to make Gin-Yung as happy as she can be. She doesn't need your pity, just your support. Do you understand what I'm saying?"

Todd nodded weakly. "Yes."

"Do you mean it?" Kim's voice had lost its hard edge and her eyes were weary. "I swear, Todd, if you can't do this, then don't even bother."

Todd felt as if he had just taken his last step on solid ground and was about to hurl himself into a black abyss. And he was almost willing to take the plunge—almost. "It's all right, Kim," he said. "I'll do it."

Chapter Three

"Our only witness changed her story? Just like that?" Nick Fox paced the gray-tiled floor of the police precinct and pulled at his tousled brown hair in frustration. "How could that happen?"

"It happens every day with these mob cases," Chief Wallace answered flatly, folding his hands across his broad belly. "All it takes is a couple of threats, and they'll jump through flaming hoops to get out of testifying."

"But I worked *six months* on that case!"

Chief Wallace shrugged, seemingly unimpressed. "I've seen some of my best men work on cases for years, and with no convictions to show for it either. I hate to break it to you, Fox, but you're not the only martyr around here."

Nick clenched his jaw, the tendons in his neck bulging. "There's no way I'm spending any more time on this one—it's a simple, clear-cut case. I'll have the D.A. subpoena the witness. We'll keep her under police protection until the trial."

The police chief stared at Nick through dull, half-closed eyes. "You can drag a witness onto the stand, but you can't force her to cooperate," he said dryly. "I suggest you review your paperwork and find some new leads."

Nick wearily closed his deep green eyes. *I already have too many cases to work on,* he thought tiredly. *I don't have time for this.* It was days like this that Nick fantasized about leaving his job as an undercover cop; sweeping up his girlfriend, Jessica, in his arms; and settling down with her in a small, quiet town near the ocean. In his mind's eye Nick could see them in a cozy bungalow with a tiny backyard and a happy golden retriever frolicking on the lawn. Nick would go back to school, and Jessica would welcome him home every night with passionate kisses and an elegant dinner. Together they would have a blissful, peaceful life.

Yeah, right, Nick thought, smirking inwardly at his own fantasy. The reality was that Jessica was more suited to beachfront estates than bungalows and energetic cities instead of sleepy little towns. And she didn't know the first thing about turning on an oven, let alone cooking a meal. Jessica craved constant excitement—for her, settling down would be the same as a jail sentence.

Maybe I just need a few days off, Nick thought, taking a seat on the captain's vinyl couch. The muscles in his shoulders and back had tied themselves into ropy knots. His entire body begged for rest—a few video rentals, some takeout, and Jessica by his side was all he needed to recharge his batteries.

"Look, Captain." Nick sighed. "I was thinking that maybe I—"

Bill Fagen suddenly appeared in the doorway, sliding on his gun holster, his brow creased with urgency. "Nick—," he interrupted, stepping into the captain's office. "We just got a tip about a car chop operation on the other side of town. I'm heading over there right now."

Good-bye, vacation, Nick whispered to himself. "Do you want me to go with you?"

Bill shook his head. "I'm just going to check out the tip to see if it's for real. If there's anything there, we'll set up a sting."

Nick exhaled. He was off the hook—for the moment.

"While you're waiting for Bill, there's a new case that's just come in that I'd like you to take a look at," the captain said, pushing an overstuffed file folder across his desk. "Take it easy,

Bill. If something shady is going down, we want to take them by surprise."

"Right, Captain," Bill answered, throwing on his jean jacket. "Hey, Nick, could you do me a favor?"

"Sure—what is it?" Nick asked. Bill had done many favors for him in the past, and he didn't feel right about saying no.

"There's a hubcap I special-ordered for my vintage T-bird. It took me almost a year to track it down. I finally hooked up with a dealership who found it for me, but there's no way I can make it over there today. Do you think you could wing over and pick it up?"

"No problem," Nick answered.

"Thanks, man. But be careful with it," Bill said. "That hubcap cost me a bundle."

"I'll take good care of it," he said as Bill rushed off. Nick's shoulders sagged as he flipped through the contents of the folder. It was enough paperwork to keep him busy into the next year.

"You'd better get going," Captain Wallace said, pointing to the folder. "You've got a lot of work to do."

Nick stood up. Holding the enormous file in his arms, he slunk back to his dingy little cubicle. "Just another day at the precinct," he muttered to himself as he dropped the file on his desk with a less than satisfying thud.

*   *   *

Gin-Yung felt as if she were floating. It wasn't the light feeling of being supported on a cushion of air, nor was it the buoyant sensation of water. With her eyes closed and her head tilted back, Gin-Yung imagined herself suspended in a thick, jellylike atmosphere, the sluggish substance seeping into her mouth, her ears, her nose, and her veins. It was around her and in her, pinning her to the bed and holding her up at the same time. Occasionally it pushed her up, as if she were coming out of water for a breath of air, and in those moments Gin-Yung came back to her family.

She had that sensation now, rising out of the ooze, shades of gray metamorphosing into patches of color. Small sounds were coming in— voices—the words too muffled and bubbly sounding for her to understand. Gin-Yung's eyes opened enough to allow her gaze to fall on hazy pots of roses and wildflowers. *I'm in a garden,* she thought groggily. *I'm in a beautiful garden . . . what a perfect place to be. . . .*

Gin-Yung's eyes closed once again, and she let herself sink back into the thick, murky pool. As she began to drift off, the sound of her mother's voice sliced through the depths.

"Todd! You're back," her mother said. "I thought you were finally going to go home and get some sleep."

Then Gin-Yung heard Todd's voice, low and smooth, touched with a hint of sadness. It rolled over her like a cool wave. "I just went for some coffee. I'll go in a little while," he said.

"You should go now," Gin-Yung's mom insisted. "She's sleeping right now. It would be the perfect time."

No, it wouldn't, Gin-Yung thought suddenly, pushing for her senses to come alive. *I want to be with Todd now.* She fought against the dampness that held her under, out of Todd's reach. *I have to see him. . . . I need you, Todd.*

Then, like a bubble rising to the surface, Gin-Yung broke through. As she began to return to full consciousness the pain returned, like thousands of hot needles pricking each one of her nerve endings. Every inch of her body ached and burned—her arms and legs, the back of her neck, her knuckles, her earlobes, her toes, even the hair follicles on her closely cropped head. As Gin-Yung's entire being screamed with sensitivity she tried to remember what it was like when she had been comfortable inside her own body. It seemed hard to believe that she could once walk, talk, sit up, and breathe without even trying.

Gin-Yung opened her eyes as wide as she could and slowly realized that she had mistaken several bouquets of roses and floral arrangements for a garden. Sluggishly and painfully she turned her sore head to the other side of the room, and her family came into view. Everyone was there. Grandmother was sitting in a chair, holding Gin-Yung's pretty little seven-year-old sister, Chung-Hee. Her teenage brother, Byung-Wah, was leaning against the wall, looking down at the floor. Her father was polishing his dark-rimmed glasses on his short-sleeved dress shirt. Kim was looking absently out the window. Her mother's short, round little body could barely be seen; she was talking to Todd and was dwarfed by his tall, muscular frame. The scene was so simple and yet so beautiful that it made Gin-Yung want to cry. *I'm going to miss them all so much,* she realized.

"Please, Todd." Her mother was still trying to convince him to leave. "You need to have a good meal and some rest. Byung-Wah—," she called to Gin-Yung's brother. "See if you can find Todd a sandwich in the basket."

Byung-Wah dutifully opened the family's picnic basket and searched through it. "Nothing left," he said sullenly.

That's just like my mom, Gin-Yung thought in mild amusement. *Always taking care of everyone.*

Now Mr. Suh was getting into the act. "Go home and sleep," he said to Todd. "Gin probably won't be awake until you get back."

43

"I'm awake now," Gin-Yung said weakly, pulling aside her respirator tube. Everyone turned to her. Bracing her hand against the metal bars on the right side of the bed, Gin-Yung tried to pull herself up a little so she could see everyone better, but the muscles in her arm didn't seem to be working. She concentrated hard—*How did I used to do it?*—but her body wouldn't move the way she wanted it to.

"My baby!" Gin-Yung's mom rushed over and tucked an extra pillow behind her daughter's head. "Is that better?"

"It's fine. Thanks, Mother," Gin-Yung breathed, her back aching from the sudden change in position.

Todd smiled and waved at her from the foot of the bed. "Good morning, Gin," he said. "How are you feeling?"

"Wonderful, now that you're here," Gin-Yung answered.

Todd gripped the foot of the bed nervously, his knees buckling beneath him. He was surrounded by Gin-Yung's entire family. Todd's shoulders sagged under the pressure of their stares. A feeling of reserved hope hovered around him, as if the Suh family had collectively decided that Gin-Yung needed a friend by her side—someone to make her happy and maybe even help her get well again. And Todd seemed to be the one they had chosen.

Why me? In a daze Todd stared down at the orange blanket covering Gin-Yung's bed. His stomach turned somersaults. He was flattered that they thought he'd be good for Gin-Yung, but Todd really didn't want the job. *Why now?* Everything in his life had been going along so well and then *boom!*—something like this hit him. He and Elizabeth were back together now, and he was busy with classes and the team. . . . *It's not that I don't want Gin-Yung to get better,* Todd explained silently. *It's just that I don't really have the time.*

But you made a promise, a little voice in the back of Todd's mind reminded him. *You're in too deep to back out of it now.*

Kim moved away from the window and walked past Todd. "Get closer," she hissed as she walked by. "Talk to her."

Inhaling deeply, Todd walked over to the wooden chair next to Gin-Yung's bed and flashed a pained smile at the family. He felt as if he were a circus animal, expected to perform on cue.

"Let's go get some lunch, everybody!" Kim suddenly announced as if she actually wanted to make things easier for him. She waved everyone toward the hallway, like a tour guide directing her group. "We'd better be quick—the cafeteria special today is egg salad sandwiches. If we don't get there soon, they might be all gone!"

"But it's only eleven-thirty," Mrs. Suh complained, lagging behind the others. "Gin-Yung's awake. She needs company."

"Don't worry about that," Kim answered as she pulled at her mother's hand. "She has Todd now." She gave her sister a sly wink.

Gin-Yung smiled. "I'll be all right, Mom. Go and have something to eat."

After a moment's hesitation Gin-Yung's mother nodded and followed her family out the door. "We'll be back soon," she called.

"Bye, guys!" Kim called brightly. But Todd caught a glimpse of her penetrating stare just as she was leaving, her dark eyes narrowing fiercely as if to say, *Remember what I told you. Don't you dare let her down.*

Gin-Yung sighed when they all had left. "It's so terrible to be adored," she said jokingly.

Todd didn't know what to say. He folded his arms awkwardly across his lap, eyes glued to the hypnotic pulses of the heart monitor. For every beep there was a tense fraction of a second when there was the possibility that another one might not come. But then it did, and the anxiety started all over again. *What if something happens while I'm alone with her?*

Todd wondered. The thought chilled him to the core.

"You look tired," Gin-Yung said, rolling her head to face him. "Kim said you slept in the waiting room last night."

"Yeah." Todd wiped his sweaty palms on the front of his jeans. "I'm going to go home and catch a little shut-eye later." Then, remembering Kim's ground rules, he said, "I'll come back tonight. Is there anything you want me to bring for you?"

Gin-Yung's eyes fixed on the ugly blue-and-white hospital gown she was wearing. "How about a new wardrobe?" she suggested sarcastically. "Something chic to go with my new hairdo."

Todd tore his eyes away from the monitor and looked into Gin-Yung's eyes. They were soft and liquid, but there was still a hint of mischief lurking there. She was trying to break the ice for him. A small, grateful smile parted his lips.

"Hey—I *like* that new hairdo," Todd answered, pointing to the top of her stubbly head. "It's *very* hip right now. Half the guys on the Lakers are wearing it."

Gin-Yung laughed so hard, tears streamed down her cheeks. Todd laughed too, gently, relieved that he had said something right. *Maybe*

47

the trick is to act like nothing's wrong, Todd thought. *Maybe I should try to talk to her just like I used to.* If he tried really hard, Todd knew he could convince himself that Gin-Yung wasn't sick, that she had at least another fifty years left. He could pretend, at least for a little while.

"Seriously, though," Todd said, trying to block out the tubes and equipment surrounding her. "If there's anything you need, I'll take care of it. Just say the word."

"I can't think of anything right now," Gin-Yung answered, quickly wiping away tears of laughter that could just as easily have been tears of sorrow. "But I'll let you know if I do."

An idea sparked inside Todd's mind. *Maybe I don't have to do this all alone,* he realized. *Gin has lots of friends.* Todd leaned forward a little. "Maybe I could bring some of your friends here so they could visit with you too."

Gin-Yung shook her head slowly, her smile fading. "Please don't, Todd. I don't want anyone to see me like this."

"I understand," Todd murmured, pursing his lips thoughtfully. He was about to ask Gin-Yung if her boyfriend in London knew about her illness, but then he suddenly remembered what Kim had said—that Gin-Yung had lied about having a new boyfriend so that Todd would stay with Elizabeth. *Ask her yourself,* Kim had said.

Curiosity smoldered inside him. *I have to know the truth.*

"But what about your boyfriend in London?" Todd asked carefully, not wanting to ask her outright if she'd lied. "Has anyone called and told him yet? Maybe it would be really good for you to have him here."

Gin-Yung sheepishly looked away. "Todd, I have a confession to make—there is no boyfriend in London."

"No?" Todd swallowed hard, his throat aching. *Kim was right after all.* Todd held his head in his hands and tried to make sense of it all.

"No," Gin-Yung answered firmly. "He doesn't exist. I made him up." Her eyes rolled up to the white ceiling, corners of eyes wet with fresh tears. "I thought if I told you there was someone else, it would be easier for you to go back to Elizabeth." She took in a shaky breath of air. "Elizabeth is a wonderful person. I feel good about leaving you with her."

Gin-Yung's words pierced Todd's protective shell and touched his heart. The selflessness of her act both baffled and moved him. "Gin-Yung—" Todd's voice cracked as he felt a surprising mist of tears springing to his own eyes. "I can't believe you were thinking of me at a time like this. . . ."

"I'm *always* thinking of you," Gin-Yung answered, and her pale cheeks flushed slightly with a touch of color. "I'm sorry I lied to you, Todd. There's never been anyone else—it's always been you."

Cold, numbing shame slid like an ice cube down Todd's throat and settled in the hollow of his chest. Had Gin-Yung always been so giving of herself? Why hadn't he noticed it before? Had his undying love for Elizabeth blinded Todd to what had been right in front of him? Todd felt as if he'd grossly shortchanged her without even being aware of it. Gin-Yung had been giving Todd her all, and he had been giving her whatever was convenient.

Todd hesitantly reached over and covered Gin-Yung's hand with his. Her fingers were bony and cold.

"I have another confession to make," she whispered.

"What is it?" Todd asked.

Gin-Yung squeezed his hand with seemingly every last ounce of strength she had. "I'm scared, Todd. I'm *so* scared."

"So am I, Gin-Yung," Todd murmured, caressing the back of her hand. "So am I."

"How could you be in love with my girlfriend?" Tom's voice broke as he pounded his fist on his father's desk. A coffee-stained photograph of Elizabeth stuck to his hand and Tom flung it off, repulsed. "How could you betray your own son?"

Mr. Conroy hung his head in apparent shame. "You have to believe me when I tell you I never wanted it to happen."

Tom grabbed a fistful of wet photos and thrust them in Mr. Conroy's face. "Look at these! What is wrong with you? Elizabeth's half your age, George, and you're spying on her like an obsessed lunatic!"

"I can imagine how wrong it must seem to you—but sometimes things just happen that we have no control over," Mr. Conroy said, his voice trembling. He buried his face in his hands.

The fire that scorched Tom's insides was building to a fever pitch. He stepped away from the desk and tore around the room in dizzying circles—around the desk, along the wall, looping back around the couch—afraid that if he stopped, he might just explode.

"You are a grown man, George, not some kid who doesn't know any better," Tom countered. "Don't tell me you had no control over your emotions. Elizabeth was my *girlfriend*. What you did was *sick!*"

"But Tom, I knew Elizabeth before I knew you were my son." Deep lines appeared on

George's forehead and around his eyes, making him look far older than he actually was. "We met in the bursar's office—"

"I don't want to hear this," Tom interrupted, waving him off.

"*Please,* Tom. Please hear me out."

Tom stopped dead in his tracks, feet spread apart in a defensive stance. "Go ahead. At this point nothing else could shock me."

"We met in the bursar's office," Mr. Conroy repeated weakly. "This was when I first came to town to try and find you. The person at the desk was having trouble coming up with any information for me. That's when I noticed a beautiful young woman—"

"No. I *definitely* don't want to hear this." Tom threw up his hands and walked over to the window. He looked out and tried to concentrate on the cars passing by below. *Blue minivan. Red Camaro. Gold Coupe de Ville,* he rattled off anxiously, hoping his father's words wouldn't reach him.

But Mr. Conroy pressed on. "Here I was, a perfect stranger, and Elizabeth suddenly introduces herself to me, volunteering to help me locate my lost son. Such kindness is not something you encounter every day." He drew in a quaking breath. "Of course she was smart and beautiful and talented—but I knew my place. Yet as the days passed, when we were working so closely with each other, I found myself becoming hopelessly taken with her. She's an exquisite girl."

Tom whirled around angrily. "I know all of those things about Elizabeth, George. And you took all of them away from me."

Seemingly unfazed, Mr. Conroy stopped to pour himself a glass of water from a carafe on the corner of his desk. "When at last we'd found you, I was ecstatic, of course. It just happened to be an unfortunate coincidence that my long-lost son was also the boyfriend of this amazing woman."

"Unfortunate coincidence?" Tom repeated, appalled. "As soon as you knew we were dating, your . . . *feelings* for Elizabeth should've stopped cold. Period." Tom smacked a clenched fist into his open palm for emphasis, his voice dripping with resentment. "Only a *freak* would do what you did."

Tom's last sentence hung in the air and fell with sharp precision, hitting its mark like the blade of a guillotine. Mr. Conroy slumped over in his desk chair, face reddening, his eyes brimming with tears.

"I tried to forget about her—believe me, I did—but the three of us were spending so much time together," Mr. Conroy cried. "I tried so hard . . . but I couldn't help it. I was so weak."

"You should've tried *harder!*" Tom's voice pounded against the office walls. He closed his eyes and tried to rub away the headache that throbbed in his temples. "What kills me about this whole thing was that Elizabeth told me repeatedly that you had come on to her, and I didn't believe her! I thought she was lying! I thought—you *told* me—that she was jealous of my new relationship with you!"

Tears poured from the corners of Mr. Conroy's eyes. "I'm so sorry, Tom. . . ."

"Elizabeth was *horrified* that you tried to kiss her." Tom spit out the words like venom, knowing that telling Mr. Conroy how Elizabeth truly felt about him would do the most damage to his father's heart. "You never, *ever* had a chance with her!"

Mr. Conroy winced, and Tom instantly knew the poison had sunk in. Remorse flickered briefly inside Tom's chest, like a dying flame, only to be extinguished by the realization that his father's actions might have cost him Elizabeth—forever.

"Elizabeth was the only woman I've ever loved." Tom clenched his jaw to fight back the tears. "And you took her away from me."

"But you have Dana now, Tom. You told me

you were in love with her. Can't we forget about all this and start over?"

The mention of Dana Upshaw's name unnerved Tom. Dana was a smart, sweet woman, but she wasn't Elizabeth. Now that Tom knew the truth, he had no idea where exactly Dana fit into the chaos. What he did know, more than anything, was that his entire being yearned to be in Elizabeth's arms again, to tell her how sorry he was for not believing her.

Is there any chance Elizabeth could forgive me? Tom wondered in silent agony. *Or is it over between us for good?*

The pain in Tom's heart ignited into a ball of fury. "I don't want to start over!" he shouted. "I want things to be the way they were before I met you! I'd rather have no father at all than a lying creep!"

"I know I'm weak." Mr. Conroy's voice was thin and reedy, his eyes pleading. "But our relationship is the most important thing in the world to me, Tom. I don't want to lose you again."

Tom turned away and headed for the door, unable to watch the man he had so admired crumble in defeat. "You already have," he said quietly.

Chapter Four

"Look out, Nick! I'm coming to save you!" Jessica shouted to the warm breeze that whipped through her golden hair as she maneuvered the red Jeep through heavy midtown traffic. It was a perfect California day—too beautiful to be wasted on dull classes indoors. After she had canceled all her afternoon lectures due to lack of interest, Jessica had a brilliant idea. She'd go to the precinct and kidnap Nick so they could spend the rest of the day together.

Just wait until you see what I have planned for you, Detective Fox. Jessica's glossy pink lips parted in a sly smile. As she waited for the traffic light to change she tapped her perfectly manicured fingertips on the steering wheel in time to the Caribbean music playing on the radio.

The dream she'd had of being stranded on

an island with Nick had inspired her. As soon as she dragged him away from his work, they'd get some mangoes and coconuts and head for the beach for a full afternoon on the water—windsurfing, boating, whatever. One thing was for sure: Jessica was hungry for some excitement.

The light turned green, but traffic was at a standstill. Jessica honked her horn. "Get moving, you slowpokes!" she shouted out the window. "I've got a boyfriend to kidnap!" The cars ahead of her crept along, inch by inch, like one giant, moving parking lot.

Jessica moaned. She knew the traffic jam was an omen. "What else is going to go wrong?" she hissed through gritted teeth. Then, as if to answer her, Jessica caught sight of the flashing blue lights of the police cruiser behind her. The officer was waving at her to pull over.

"Grrreat," Jessica muttered, her lips drawn into a tight line as she pulled the Jeep over into the breakdown lane. "What's he going to charge me with, speeding?"

The officer stepped out of the car and walked slowly over to Jessica's open window. Jessica's stern expression faded when the officer lifted his mirrored sunglasses and smiled at her. It was one of Nick's buddies from the Sweet Valley precinct.

"Hey, Ronny!" Jessica flashed him a

charming smile. "I didn't know you guys gave out tickets for driving too slow."

"We don't," Ronny McAllister said with a grin. "But I *am* required to inform you that your left brake light is out."

"Oh yeah?"

The officer leaned casually against the Jeep. "You have to get the bulb replaced as soon as you can. I'm sure Nick wouldn't want his girlfriend driving around in a dangerous vehicle."

"Nick could fix it for me . . . if only I could get to him." She looked up at the line of cars crawling past and ran the back of her hand across her forehead melodramatically. "Traffic is just *vicious* today."

Ronny put his sunglasses back on. "You're heading to the station?"

Jessica nodded flirtatiously, glancing again at the blue dome lights reflected in her rearview mirror. She had a brilliant idea, and she wasn't about to let it slide. "Say, Ronny, how'd you like to help out your buddy's girlfriend?"

"No problem. But only if you get that bulb changed, pronto," he said.

"It's a deal."

Two minutes later, after a minimum of smooth talk, Jessica found herself out of stalled traffic and in the freeway's breakdown lane. She coasted past the miles of parked cars, thanks to

Ronny's "police escort" in front of her. She'd asked Ronny to go the whole nine yards, just for fun, and he'd agreed; his blue dome lights whirled and flashed, and he even let out an occasional siren blast.

Jessica felt like a true VIP. She waved and blew kisses to the outraged drivers as if she were a beauty pageant queen on a parade float. "Ciao, darling!" she called to a red-faced businessman who punched the steering wheel of his flashy Alfa Romeo angrily as she sped by him. "Too bad you don't have friends in high places!"

The ride to the police station was a short one—almost *too* short, in Jessica's opinion. She was having the time of her life.

"Hey, Nick!" Ronny shouted as he led Jessica into the detectives' room. "Guess who I just picked up out there."

Nick was leaning against his desk, muscles rippling beneath his black T-shirt. Nick's deep green eyes sent a shivery thrill down Jessica's spine, and his full, sexy lips were puckered slightly. It took all Jessica's self-control not to hurtle over the other desks in her path and wrap herself around Nick's spectacular biceps.

"Oh, Jess, what did you do now?" Nick said with a groan. Worry lines formed over his brow.

Jessica arched one perfect eyebrow. "What

makes you think I did something wrong?"

"Because I *know* you—"

Ronny interrupted Nick with a pat on the back before he headed out of the detectives' area. "Brake light was out, that's all," he said reassuringly.

Nick's smile returned. "Get over here, beautiful."

"I guess Detective Fox wants to have a word with me," Jessica purred, playfully licking her lips. The dimple in her left cheek made a sudden appearance as she sauntered over to Nick's desk. She thanked her lucky stars that Nick was an undercover cop and not a uniformed policeman like the others; with a body like his, it would've been a shame to put him in anything but the faded, formfitting jeans he wore so well.

"Just a bulb, huh?" Nick rubbed the dark stubble on his unshaven jaw and shot her a mischievous grin. "I was afraid you'd been caught doing some more freelance undercover work."

Jessica rolled her eyes. "Give me some credit, Nick," she said, pressing her hands against his strong chest as she pushed him back behind the divider that separated his desk from the other detectives'.

Nick snaked his arms around Jessica's waist and stared at her thoughtfully. "So you've learned your lesson?"

Jessica's perfectly manicured hands traveled up Nick's sinewy arms and came to rest on his broad shoulders. "For the time being," she answered coyly.

"You really wear me out, Jessica Wakefield," Nick whispered huskily in her ear. He kissed Jessica lightly on the earlobe, then followed a tender trail along her jaw until he found her waiting mouth. They kissed passionately for several minutes, unfazed by the fact that they could get walked in on at any moment. But no one walked in.

"So," Nick said, kissing Jessica chastely on the tip of the nose. "How's my favorite calendar girl been?"

"I've been OK," Jessica answered lightly, twirling a strand of golden blond hair around her fingers. Between Elizabeth's boyfriend angst and Nick's tight jeans, Jessica had nearly forgotten about her upcoming photo shoot. She had won a contest to model for a charity calendar with Bobby Hornet, the famous rock singer. Not only was the sexy bikini calendar going to be used to raise money for the homeless, but it was also the perfect stepping-stone for Jessica's dream career of becoming a model. Unlike the way most boyfriends would have behaved, Nick had been incredibly supportive, further confirming Jessica's theory that he was The Best Boyfriend in the World.

Jessica sat down on the edge of Nick's desk, her knees still weak from his kiss. "Life's been pretty grim at my place, though. With my exams and Gin-Yung dying and all . . ."

"Who's Gin-Yung?" Nick's brow suddenly wrinkled in concern.

Jessica waved dismissively. "You know what? I don't really feel like talking about that right now. It's too depressing." She jumped off the desk. "The bottom line is that I need some excitement in my life." Sending Nick a sideways glance, Jessica eyed him slyly. "Maybe I should quit school and become an undercover narc."

"Jess . . . you said you learned your lesson," Nick said seriously, taking a seat behind the enormous stacks of paper that littered his desk.

"I was only joking," Jessica argued, resting her hands firmly on her hips. "Boy, are you tense."

"Sorry," Nick said with a wilted smile. "I have a lot on my mind."

Jessica walked around behind Nick's chair and began kneading his tense shoulders with her fingertips. Nick lowered his head and groaned appreciatively.

"It does sound kind of cool, though, doesn't it?" Jessica said.

"What sounds cool?"

"You know, me becoming a narc," Jessica said wistfully. "We could fight crime together, Nick. We'd be the hottest team to ever hit the streets."

"Somebody's been watching too many cop shows on TV." Nick lifted his head and turned to her. "I don't know what it's going to take to make you understand that being a narc is a very dangerous, unglamorous, and often aggravating job." He ran his hands through his rumpled brown hair, then laced his fingers behind his head. "This morning one of my key witnesses in a mob case changed her story, and now we're right back to square one. I have to spend the rest of the day pushing papers, trying to find another lead to follow."

"My poor baby," Jessica cooed sympathetically, working at a knotted muscle near his shoulder blade. "It sounds like we both need some fun and excitement tonight. Why don't we rent a Jet Ski and head for the beach at sunset? Then maybe we could go club hopping later. I've heard about this great all-night place that just opened."

Nick's broad shoulders rose and fell as he sighed heavily. "Actually, Jess, I was looking forward to something a little more quiet. Why don't we get some Chinese takeout and rent a couple of videos?"

Jessica dropped her hands to her sides, her pretty features twisted into a sour expression. She resisted the urge to stomp her feet impatiently on the floor. "Come on, Nick! Don't wimp out on me!"

"I can't do it tonight. I'm worn out. We can get a Jet Ski and go club hopping some other night." When Jessica parted her glossy lips to protest, Nick gently kissed them. "I promise."

"Oh, all right." Jessica relented. When it came to Nick's kisses, Jessica was completely defenseless.

"Thanks, honey," Nick answered gratefully. "I really appreciate it."

It's a good thing Nick is so gorgeous and sexy, Jessica thought as she resumed massaging Nick's muscular back. *At least there's always some kind of excitement to look forward to. But if Nick thinks I'm going to sit around watching videos for the rest of my life, he's got another thing coming.*

"Not again!" Elizabeth rooted through her leather backpack, hoping to find her blue Restoration poetry textbook. But her thick French book was there in its place. "I can't believe I've done this twice today," she mumbled tiredly to herself before she spun around on her sandaled heels and marched out of the austere English building into the bright midday sun.

The thought of trekking all the way across campus again filled her with bone-deep exhaustion and dread. She only had five minutes to rush back to her room and get the right book before class started.

I just can't concentrate on anything today. Elizabeth popped on a denim baseball cap and adjusted the visor to shield her eyes from the sun's rays. She seemed to be moving in slow motion, as if she were walking through water. *Maybe I'm still asleep, and this is all a bad dream,* Elizabeth hoped. *When I wake up, Todd and I will be lying on a beautiful beach on some stranded island, with nothing but coconuts, mangoes, and our love to keep us alive.* Stealing her sister's fantasy gave Elizabeth little comfort as she hurried across the grassy quad. She had her own laundry list to add. *Plus Gin-Yung will still be in London, Tom will have disappeared, and everyone will be happy.*

If only I were dreaming, Elizabeth thought ruefully. The baggy denim overalls she was wearing swished around her ankles as she walked. Why did her dorm seem so far away today? She'd never reach it and get back to class in time.

"Liz, wait up!"

Elizabeth looked up to see Todd rushing toward her. He was wearing the same rugby shirt and jeans as the day before. *Please tell me you're coming to take me away to a deserted island,* Elizabeth pleaded silently.

"Oh, Todd," Elizabeth breathed at the sight of his downcast face. He looked as if he'd aged overnight. "How is Gin-Yung?" she asked, tenderly touching the stubble on his chin.

"As well as can be expected," Todd answered heavily. His soft brown eyes stared at her for a moment, then he leaned toward Elizabeth and pressed his lips to hers in a slow, lingering kiss.

Elizabeth closed her eyes and breathed in Todd's warmth, hoping the kiss would never end. She wrapped her arms around his neck, feeling Todd's strong arms encircling her waist. They fit together so comfortably, so perfectly.

Yet in the middle of her moment of bliss, the memory of Gin-Yung nagged at the back of Elizabeth's mind. Feelings of guilt slipped in and out of her consciousness lightly and more easily than Elizabeth had expected. One minute she was thinking of Gin-Yung, and a moment later the sensation of Todd's lips on the hollow of her throat made her forget everything.

Todd pulled away slightly, his arms still wrapped around her. His eyelids drooped. "It was awful seeing her, Liz," he said hoarsely. "I almost didn't recognize her. There are all these machines and tubes . . . and she's so weak. . . ."

Her heart became heavy again. "Is she conscious?"

"She slides in and out of consciousness," he said. "I talked to her a little bit."

Elizabeth placed her palms flat against Todd's chest. "Is she scared?"

Todd nodded, parting his lips to speak but faltering before he could. Elizabeth rested her head on his chest and felt Todd's strong, clear heartbeat pound against her cheek. *We have so much more time ahead of us,* Elizabeth thought. *And Gin-Yung has none.*

"She lied about having a boyfriend, Liz," Todd whispered.

Elizabeth looked up at him uncomprehendingly. "What?"

Todd pressed his chin against her forehead. "She made him up so you and I could stay together. She said she wanted to leave me with you."

"Oh, Todd!" Elizabeth gasped. Her stomach felt like it had been dropped down an elevator shaft. *Gin-Yung sacrificed herself for him—for us.* It would've been so much easier if Gin-Yung had been selfish and unlikable. But Gin-Yung's goodness was tearing Elizabeth apart.

She looked up at Todd, her eyes watering. "It must be so horrible—I can't imagine what it's like for her."

Todd looked up at the blue sky. "I'm going back to the hospital tonight to bring her a few things. You don't mind, do you?"

"Why should I mind?" Elizabeth said with forced lightness. She clung to him to reassure herself that he was solid, afraid that he would slip through her fingers like grains of sand. It was starting already. She could feel it.

Todd's eyes welled up, and his face reddened. *He knows it's happening too.* As he brought Elizabeth's hand to his lips and kissed the tips of her fingers, a warm teardrop fell from his lashes onto her knuckle. "She needs company," he murmured, his voice breaking.

"Of course she does." The corners of Elizabeth's mouth trembled. She intertwined her fingers tightly in his, feeling his warm pulse. Digging down deep, Elizabeth pulled up the words she was afraid she wouldn't have the courage to say. "She needs you, Todd."

"I know," he whispered, his breath soft against her cheek. "It's just that . . ." Todd trailed off, falling silent. He held her close, his body trembling. "I wish I could be in two places at the same time, Liz."

Elizabeth bit the inside of her cheek to keep from bursting into tears. *But what about us?* She wanted to scream out loud and beat her fists against his chest and tell him how scared she was and cry in his arms. . . . *Stay with me!*

"Oh, Liz . . ." Todd choked back a sob, as if he read her thoughts. "Maybe this is a bad idea. I could go there tonight and tell her I can't visit her anymore. . . . I'll say good-bye."

"Don't." A stronger voice was coming from inside Elizabeth now, speaking beyond what her emotions would allow. Saying good-bye to Gin-Yung would break her heart, and they both knew it. She deserved better, as painful as it was to admit. "You go to her and take care of her, Todd. It's the right thing for us to do."

Todd cupped her face in his warm hands and stared into her blue-green eyes. "I love you more than I've ever loved anyone in my entire life." He took a deep breath. "You know that, don't you?"

Elizabeth nodded imperceptibly. "I love you too, Todd."

"Just because we're going to spend a little time apart doesn't mean we can't still love each other, right?" The rise in pitch of Todd's voice made Elizabeth wonder if he wasn't sure himself.

"Right," she answered, tearing herself away from his gaze. A dark cloud of disappointment was hanging over her. She'd worked so hard to convince him to take care of Gin-Yung, and yet it saddened her that he'd agreed with her.

Todd brushed a golden strand of blond hair out of her eyes. "It's just temporary," he said. "It's not forever."

"No, it's not." Elizabeth tried to convince herself. "It's just for a little while."

"You're so special to me, Liz." Todd tilted her face up toward his and kissed her tenderly on one cheek, then the other. His thumbs wiped away her tears. "When this is over, we'll be together again. I promise."

I want to believe you, but I don't know if I can, Elizabeth thought, trying to remind herself that what they were doing was the best thing possible for everyone.

Todd held up his hands and Elizabeth did the same, pressing hand to hand, palm to palm, finger to finger. Their eyes locked, chests rising and falling together. As Todd and Elizabeth's lips touched they breathed as one, their bodies melting together. She closed her eyes, savoring the sweetness as their kisses deepened, her senses recording every nuance imprinting itself on her permanent memory. Elizabeth wanted to remember the warmth of the heat rising up from Todd's face, the earthy scent of his skin, the brush of his rough cheek against hers, the beating of his heart, the taste of his lips. Elizabeth wanted to make it the kiss of a lifetime—just in case it was to be their last.

Chapter Five

"So you really think the concerto's going OK so far?" Dana Upshaw asked as she exited the classical arched doorway of the music building with her performance instructor, Anthony Davidovic, by her side. She expertly balanced the neck of her padded nylon cello case against her shoulder, letting the metal wheel at the bottom of the bag roll on the ground as she walked.

Anthony, SVU's youngest and newest music professor, had been tutoring Dana for several months. "It's coming along beautifully, Dana. I really mean it," he assured her, his round, intelligent gray eyes wide with enthusiasm. "This week you should concentrate on keeping the tempo even in the second movement. As soon as you have that mastered we can start working on the third section."

"I've already tried to sight-read it a little. The melody is absolutely gorgeous," Dana said, pausing briefly to rearrange her long, free-flying mahogany curls on top of her head in a funky, hand-tooled silver barrette. She sighed luxuriously as she felt the afternoon sun warm and loosen the overworked tendons in her forearms and hands. Her Tuesday afternoon practice session with Anthony had been tiring but completely fulfilling—and that was just the way she liked it. Music was her passion, and Dana wanted to immerse herself completely in the art.

"You're every teacher's dream, Dana," Anthony said with a gentle smile as they walked side by side past the administration building. "Even at the university level I have to beg most of my students to practice. And here you are—already skipping ahead!" They continued west toward the parking lot, where Anthony's car was parked.

"I've always been very driven in everything I do," she answered modestly.

"It's the only way to get ahead in this world. Persistence, drive, and talent are the keys to success, and in your case you have all three," the professor said. "If we can really get going on this piece, I was thinking we could approach the director of the SVU select orchestra about performing the concerto next semester."

"Ohmigosh! That would be incredible!" Dana was already coasting on the success of the solo she had performed with the string ensemble the previous week. But now she was so excited by the prospect of being a special guest soloist with the entire select orchestra that she nearly dropped her expensive instrument on the ground. Luckily Anthony reached out and made the save. Dana thanked him breathlessly and twisted the safety strap several times around her wrist. Her heart was bursting with excitement. "I've been dreaming of playing with them ever since I started here! I can't believe it could happen so soon."

"Wait a minute—don't get your hopes up. We don't have the gig yet," Anthony said cautiously, despite the encouraging grin on his face. "You still have a lot of practice ahead of you. Maybe we should try to fit in a few extra sessions to get you rolling. Are you free Thursday?"

"I have a lesson to teach," Dana answered after mentally running through her schedule.

"How about Saturday?"

A sly, contented smile parted Dana's full lips. "I'm seeing Tom on Saturday."

Anthony let out a low whistle. "I take it everything went well between the two of you last weekend?"

"It was perfect," Dana answered simply.

But things between them hadn't always been so easy. Dating Tom Watts had been an uphill battle from the moment they'd met, because Tom was still hung up on his old girlfriend, Elizabeth Wakefield. He had been a hard case, one that any woman a tinge less persistent than Dana would have given up on immediately. But Tom had that perfect blend of brilliance, brooding intensity, and amazing good looks that Dana found so irresistibly attractive. *Besides,* she thought proudly. *I've never been scared away by a challenge.*

And during the past weekend, after a few weeks of long, hard work, Dana finally was able to enjoy the fruits of her labor. Step by agonizing step Tom had obviously begun to come around to realize that he and Dana made a great couple. He had even borrowed his father's gold Mercedes convertible for an intimate drive along the coast. They'd had an amazing time, zooming along the edge of the Pacific, every so often pulling over to the side of the road to look at the breathtaking view. Then they'd left the car to frolic on the beach and kiss passionately in the surf . . . just like Deborah Kerr and Burt Lancaster in *From Here to Eternity,* one of Dana's favorite classic movies. Unconsciously she touched her fingers to her lips, suddenly swept up in the memory of the sweet, tender way Tom had touched her. *Yes, I did make some progress,* Dana thought, smiling inwardly. *Pretty soon Elizabeth will be out of the picture for good.*

"I could tell Tom hadn't thought about his old girlfriend for *hours* while we were together," Dana gushed to Anthony. She felt herself blushing. "It used to be that he couldn't go for more than a few minutes without staring off into space, thinking about her."

"That definitely sounds like an improvement." Anthony twirled his car keys around his finger. "I hate to sound like an old fogy, but don't let this guy get in the way of your practice, OK? You have an extraordinary talent, Dana, and you can't afford any major distractions right now."

"Au contraire, mon professeur." Dana giggled. "Love can only add richness to my playing."

Anthony shrugged. "I suppose you're right—just as long as you keep practicing. I'd hate for you to miss out on a chance to perform with the orchestra."

Just then Dana spotted Tom's car pulling into the parking lot. *Wow, Tom's lunch with his father must have been a quick one,* she calculated silently. *Maybe he just couldn't wait to get back to campus and see me again.* With that thought Dana's heart fluttered as if it had butterfly's wings, the way it always felt whenever Tom was near her.

"Don't worry, Anthony," Dana said, unable to take her eyes off Tom's strong, gorgeous body as he stepped out of the car. "Whenever I put my mind to something, there's nothing in the world that can stop me."

Tom slammed the car door shut, his head swimming in confusion. The roiling anger that had consumed him in Mr. Conroy's office had given way to a flood of conflicting emotions that now tore at every inch of him.

Not so long ago Tom's life had come together perfectly, like the pieces of an interlocking puzzle. Elizabeth, Mr. Conroy, and his newfound half siblings, Mary and Jake, all shared a part of who Tom was, filling in the emptiness that had been inside him, making him a complete person again. *But George had to ruin it,* Tom thought bitterly as he walked toward the edge of the parking lot, ferociously kicking at the stray pebbles in his path. It was as if Tom's father had taken all the pieces of his life and thrown them carelessly in the air, letting them fall in jumbled disarray. Tom had no clue how to make the pieces fit together again. All he knew was that there was a gaping hole in his heart where they had once been.

Tom shoved his hands deep into his pockets and trudged on, his head falling to his chest. The air Tom breathed felt thick and heavy as the haunting memory of the cruel things he'd said about Elizabeth tormented him like sinister ghosts.

She's nothing but a liar. . . . If you don't watch your back, she'll put a knife in it. . . . She may look sweet and innocent, but Elizabeth Wakefield is poison. . . .

Tom cringed under an oppressive cloud of guilt. How could he have said such nasty things about someone as sweet and wonderful as Elizabeth? How could he have even believed those things in the first place? *If only I could erase all the pain I've caused her,* he thought with deep regret. Tom would have given anything in the world for Elizabeth's forgiveness, but he knew he didn't deserve it. Even if Elizabeth had somehow found it in her heart to forgive Tom for the vicious remarks he'd made, she'd never be able forget the terrible things he'd said to her on the day they broke up.

You're not the person I thought you were. . . . You've betrayed me. . . . I can't ever forgive you or trust you again. . . .

The chilling irony of Tom's own words made him shudder violently—those were the very same words Elizabeth had every right to say to *him.*

"Tom!"

The sound of a woman's voice calling his name snapped Tom out of his trance. *Is it Elizabeth?* he wondered anxiously.

Jerking up his head, he turned around abruptly. A sharp intake of breath instantly filled his lungs with expectant air. But instead of seeing the sweet, angelic face of Elizabeth, Tom looked up to see Dana's seductive curves, clad in a clingy plaid jumper, making their way toward him. Her knee-high Dr. Martens sprayed gravel behind them as she excitedly sped up her pace.

Previously Tom had found her oddball sense of style strangely enticing. But now, to him, Dana simply looked like a demented exaggeration of a Catholic schoolgirl. His heart sank.

"Great timing! I just finished my lesson," Dana chirped when she met him at his car, all smiles. Her hazel eyes sparkled sultrily.

I just can't handle talking to Dana right now, Tom thought, reacting with a slight flinch as Dana reached out to touch him fondly on the arm. Squinting, Tom watched Dana through the gray fog of confusion swarming in his head, as if he'd just met her for the first time. *Who is this beautiful woman who has suddenly wormed her way into my life? What exactly does she mean to me?* he wondered urgently. Dana might be bright, independent, artistic, and fun—but why wasn't any of that enough to satisfy him?

"Tom?" Dana waved her hand in front of his face. "Tom, is something wrong?"

Tom's chest rose and fell heavily as he sighed. He knew it would be a struggle to crawl outside of himself long enough to have a conversation with her. "I had a fight with my father," he answered distractedly.

"You poor thing," Dana cooed with sympathy. She wheeled the cello around and fell into step beside him. "What happened?"

"I really don't feel like talking about it." Tom fought to smooth out the rough edges in his voice.

"Come on, you can tell me."

Tom ran his hands through his hair. "No, really, I don't want to get into it."

Dana stopped and turned toward Tom, stroking his face with the back of her long fingers. "Was he angry that we borrowed his car?" She pouted her lips into a tantalizing pucker, as if she wanted to kiss him. "I'll call him if you want and tell him it was all my fault. I'll say I talked you into it."

"He wasn't angry about the car," Tom replied, straining to maintain the little patience he had left. The way Dana blatantly used pouting and flirting tactics to pump him for information severely grated on his nerves—Elizabeth never would've even dreamed of acting like that.

You're not being fair, whispered a tiny voice inside his head. *Dana and Elizabeth are two very different people. You can't expect them to act the same way.*

Reluctantly Tom managed a crooked smile. "Look, Dana. Can we please change the subject?"

"All right," Dana relented, sounding slightly irritated herself. She reached behind her head and unclipped the silver barrette that held back her hair. The long, dark curls tumbled over her shapely shoulders. Even in his depressed state Tom couldn't help noticing how beautiful and sexy she was. His grin became somewhat less reluctant.

Dana smiled again, apparently pleased that Tom was paying a little bit more attention to her. "I had a great time at the beach," she said, her voice as smooth as velvet. "I've really missed you since then."

"Yeah." Tom exhaled loudly, not wanting to add the customary *me too* to the equation.

"What do you mean, *yeah?*" Dana asked, her eyes narrowing. "Yeah, you had a good time, or yeah, you missed me too?"

Oh no. What does she want from me anyway? Tom suddenly felt as if he'd stuck his head in a vise and Dana was turning it tighter and tighter. Yes, he'd enjoyed going to the beach with her, but Tom couldn't say that he'd actually missed her. Wanting Elizabeth back again gave Tom new insight and perspective on the time he'd spent with Dana. He was beginning to realize that although he had fun when he was with her and enjoyed her company, the spark that had ignited was out—at least for him. Tom had *wanted* to be in love with Dana, but in retrospect he was beginning to see that she had been more of a diversion—a way for him to cope with the loss of his true love.

Dana's expectant eyes were glued to Tom, waiting for his answer. Tom swallowed hard, torn between saying what Dana wanted to hear and telling her the truth. Disgusted with the way he'd broken up with Elizabeth, Tom made a silent vow to himself not to do the same to Dana.

"Yeah," Tom answered cautiously. "Both." He groaned inwardly, knowing that Dana was too clever to be satisfied with such a pat answer.

"No, don't say 'both'—say, 'Dana, I had a great time at the beach and I missed you too.' Come on, let me hear you say the words."

"I'm not really in the mood for games," Tom said lightly, trying to wriggle out of her snare.

Dana rolled her eyes. "You're not very romantic today."

"I told you—I'm not feeling too well, and I've got a lot on my mind. There's a ton of work I need to do at the station."

"Well, if you're feeling up to it, I thought maybe we could hit the beach again on Sunday," Dana said, linking her arm in his.

The hopeful tone in her voice made Tom shudder. "I don't think so. . . ." He trailed off.

"What do you mean?" Dana's dark eyebrows knitted together.

Tom pulled his hands out of his pockets and tore his eyes away from hers, breaking the link between them.

"We can do something else—whatever you want," she said suddenly.

"I think I need a little time to myself this weekend, Dana."

"OK," she said, still persistent. "We don't have to get together on both days. But we're still on for Saturday night, right?"

Tom shook his head vigorously. "I don't know, Dana. . . ."

Tiny lines formed around Dana's eyes. "I think I'm starting to get the picture here," she said slowly.

"Things are really confusing for me right now. . . ."

"If you need a little space, I can understand that," Dana answered, fixing him with a mesmerizing stare. "But when you're alone, Tom, I want you to think about the way the ocean air smelled that day when we were together. I want you to think about how it felt to run through the hot sand and how much fun we had when we fell together in the surf. Think about how you kissed me that day, and I guarantee things will seem a lot clearer to you."

As Tom silently watched Dana walk away, he knew that she was right. *We did have a great time together, Dana,* Tom replied silently as he thought back to that day at the beach. *But I'm sorry—I still love Elizabeth. Even more now than ever.*

Chapter Six

"Which one do you like better?" Jessica held out a clingy little red number in one hand, then a revealing little blue one in the other. "I can't decide."

Elizabeth rolled her eyes and snapped her textbook shut. One of the annoyingly inescapable duties of being Jessica's sister and roommate was acting as fashion consultant when Jessica went out—which was nearly every single night. "For goodness' sake, Jess, you're only going to Nick's to watch movies. Why don't you just throw on a pair of jeans and a T-shirt? That's what I'd do."

Jessica gave her sister's baggy denim overalls the once-over and arched one perfect eyebrow in disdain. "Need I say more?"

"Fine," Elizabeth snapped, raising her hands in surrender. "Then don't ask!"

"*Somebody's* tense tonight," Jessica said in a singsong voice. She shoved the two dresses back into her messy closet and picked out a black-and-white-print halter dress and a sexy pair of strappy sandals.

"Well, I have a good reason . . . ," Elizabeth said, softer this time. She paced their small dorm room in her pink socks, restlessly straightening everything in sight. "Todd and I decided to cool things off so he can take care of Gin-Yung."

Jessica frowned. "You didn't—"

"We had to, Jess," Elizabeth argued. "We decided it was the best thing for now."

"*Who* decided?"

"We both did," Elizabeth answered. She shuddered as she relived their last kiss out on the quad. "It was so hard, Jess."

Jessica zipped the back of her dress, then gave her sister a huge hug. "I'm sorry this had to happen, Liz," she said, handing Elizabeth a tissue.

"So am I," Elizabeth said, wiping her nose.

Jessica walked over to the telephone. "Look, if you need someone to talk to tonight, I'll call Nick and cancel. We can always watch videos to-morrow night."

Elizabeth shook her head furiously. "Don't, Jess. I'll be fine . . . honest."

Jessica shot her twin a look of concern. "But what are you going to do? I know you—you'll sit around here feeling sorry for yourself. You should do something spontaneous and fun."

"This place is a mess." Elizabeth sniffled. She crossed the room and began tidying up her sock drawer. "I'll throw all my energy into straightening up. Cleaning always makes me feel better."

Her twin sister snorted. "It makes me feel better too," she said sarcastically as she tried to locate a can of hair spray in the ever present mangled pile of clothes, shoes, and beauty products that covered her bed. "After you're done playing with your socks, you should organize your colored paper clip collection."

Looking at the pairs of socks she had stacked in the same order as the colors of the rainbow, Elizabeth grabbed a yellow pair and flung them at her sister. "I wouldn't call watching videos exactly 'fun and spontaneous' either, Jess," she retorted.

Jessica dodged the flying yellow missile and gave her long blond locks a confident toss. "If I have my way, Nick will forget about having a quiet evening at home and he'll take me out for a night on the town instead," she said, dabbing perfume behind her ears. "All it will take is a little careful manipulation."

"Ha, ha. You wouldn't know anything about that, would you?" Elizabeth teased, finally understanding her sister's choice of dress. As she quickly became bored with the socks Elizabeth looked around the room for something else to do. There was nothing. The dorm room felt suffocatingly small, as if the walls were closing in on her. She slammed her sock drawer shut. "Maybe I *should* get out of here for a while," she thought aloud.

Jessica paused between coats of mascara. "I heard there's a party at Xavier Hall tonight."

"I was thinking more along the lines of watching TV down in the lounge."

Jessica batted her long, glamorous lashes. "Leave it to wild, impulsive Liz, always in pursuit of cutting-edge fun."

"*Mind-numbing* fun is really what I'm going for, but thanks for the commentary." Elizabeth headed for the door. "Good luck—and have a good time."

"Believe me, I will," Jessica said with a mischievous laugh.

Brace yourself for the longest, loneliest, saddest night of your life, Elizabeth told herself grimly as she walked out of room 28 and over to the stairwell. Her stomach was as tense as a rock. She couldn't help wondering what Todd was doing at that very moment. Was he gathering up gifts to bring to the hospital? Or was he already there, talking to Gin-Yung and holding her hand?

Stop thinking about it, she ordered herself. *You've made the right decision. Gin-Yung's last days will be happy ones. You'll never regret the choice you've made.*

"Have just a little more," Mrs. Suh coaxed, holding a spoonful of her homemade spicy noodle soup in the air above Gin-Yung's hospital bed. "It will make you stronger."

"Mom, I'm not going to get any stronger," Gin-Yung said flatly. She pressed her colorless lips together into a thin line, fighting back the feeling of panic that was continually creeping up her spine.

When are they going to stop pretending? Gin-Yung wondered silently. She was so tired of the brave faces and the chipper voices. She was tired of the forced optimism and the way everyone tip-toed around the room as if they were walking on eggshells. *Am I the only one who's accepted the fact that I'm going to die?* The idea made Gin-Yung feel even more isolated and lonely. And angry too. If Gin-Yung had the strength, she would've loved to shout at the top of her lungs to get their attention. *"Listen up!"* she'd yell until Byung-Wah, Mother and Dad, Grandmother, Kim, and even Chung-Hee all stopped their charade. *"I'm not gone yet! My body's fading, but I'm still here . . . . Don't treat me like a stranger you're afraid to talk to. Treat me the same way you did before I was sick. . . . Don't shut me out!"*

The flicker of hope that seemingly had been burning in her mother's eyes suddenly dwindled. Mrs. Suh set the bowl of soup down on the bedside table and clasped her hand to her mouth. With her chin falling against her chest, she started to cry.

"Don't talk like that, Ginny!" Chung-Hee shouted from across the room. After leaping out of Kim's lap, she skipped over to her sister's bed, her little white sneakers squeaking on the spotless floor. With a tiny cry Chung-Hee jumped up on the bed and flung her warm arms around Gin-Yung's neck. "You have to be positive, Gin. You can get well again—I *know* it."

Gin-Yung drew in a feeble breath as she touched the top of Chung-Hee's glossy black hair. Her own frail arms and cold neck contrasted starkly with the vital color and warmth of Chung-Hee's. It was as if they were completely unrelated creatures: Chung-Hee was fairy dust and sparkles, belonging to sun-drenched beaches and warm summer air, while Gin-Yung felt like a hermit crab that was withering inside its shell and slowly sinking beneath waves of cold, stinging salt water.

"Come, sit over here," Mr. Suh said to his wife, leading her away from the bed to a vinyl chair near the window. The blinds were drawn, which meant it must be nighttime, and a sliver of pink-orange light from the outside flood-lights seeped in from the bottom of the window. *Oh, how I miss going outside and smelling the fresh, clean air,* Gin-Yung thought sadly. *There are so many things I miss . . . already.*

Chung-Hee lifted her head and gave Gin-Yung a broad smile. The white flash of her sparkling teeth pleased Gin-Yung deeply. For the briefest moment she forgot about the plastic tubes running in and out of her body, the sti-fling hospital room, and the strange, burning pain that was breaking her body down piece by piece. For a moment she was free.

"Do you know what?" Chung-Hee asked coyly, starting the guessing game Gin-Yung used to play with her when she was a toddler.

"What?" Gin-Yung answered with a vague smile.

"I know someone who's going to be here soon to visit you," the sweet little girl said, giv-ing the hospital bed a small bounce.

"Who is it?"

"Well . . . let me give you a hint. . . ."

Chung-Hee looked up at the suspended ceiling as if she were deep in thought. "He's really nice and cute and he plays basketball. . . ."

"Michael Jordan," Gin-Yung teased, grinning at the outlandish idea of being visited by her favorite pro basketball player.

Kim laughed from across the room. "Sorry, sis—Michael's schedule was just too hectic. The only cute and nice basketball player available was Todd Wilkins."

"I guess he'll have to do." Gin-Yung sighed in mock exasperation. The truth was, she wouldn't have been happier if she was expecting a visit from every player in the NBA.

"I like Todd!" Chung-Hee clapped her small, delicate hands joyfully.

Gin-Yung closed her eyes. "So do I," she said. Her stomach fluttered just at the thought of seeing him again. *I love you so much, Todd,* Gin-Yung thought dreamily. *But are you visiting me because you feel you have to? Or do you really love me too?* Even though Gin-Yung couldn't help but wonder, she was afraid to know the truth. Having Todd near, for whatever reason, was simply enough for her right now.

Kim began straightening Gin-Yung's bed, tucking loose ends of the sheets under the mattress and smoothing the wrinkles out of the blankets. "He'll be here soon," she said, ushering

Chung-Hee over to where Byung-Wah was sitting. "We don't have much time to get you ready for your date, Gin."

"Kim!" Gin-Yung couldn't help laughing in spite of herself. But her deep, throaty giggles quickly deteriorated into a series of wrenching coughs. The heart monitor raced with each spasm.

Mrs. Suh rushed to her daughter's side and poured a glass of water for her. Gin-Yung drank it down, enjoying the way the cool water soothed her sore, parched throat. "I'm all right, Mother," she said when she was finally able to speak again. Her mother responded with a kiss on her forehead.

Gin-Yung smiled, hoping her harsh comment earlier hadn't hurt her mother too badly. *Let her have hope, even if it's a false one,* she told herself gently. *If it makes her feel better, that's all that matters.*

"What are you doing?" Gin-Yung asked incredulously as Kim began spritzing a misty cloud of lilac perfume over the bed.

"I already told you," she said with a wink.

"I'd hardly call this a date." Gin-Yung tugged at her embarrassing hospital gown. "I'm definitely not dressed for the occasion."

"Let's see what we can do. . . ." Kim scratched the top of her head, closed one eye, and puckered her lips, like an artist studying her canvas.

Suddenly her face brightened. "I know. . . ."

Kim strode over to Chung-Hee and whispered something in her ear. Chung-Hee softly walked over to her big brother, who was dozing in a chair, his head drooping forward. Gin-Yung watched silently, wondering what mischief her little sister was up to as she reached for the dark blue bandanna he kept tucked in the back pocket of his jeans. Stealthily she extracted the bandanna with the precision of a professional pickpocket. Byung-Wah didn't stir.

Chung-Hee giggled, covering her mouth with her hands as she handed the stolen item over to Kim. She smiled proudly, as if she'd just accomplished a tough mission and earned her stripes.

"What are you up to?" Gin-Yung whispered curiously.

"It's a head wrap for you," Kim answered. Before Gin-Yung had a chance to ask any more questions, Kim twisted the blue bandanna around her head and tied it in the back. Then she took off her gold hoop earrings and put them on Gin-Yung's ears. "Hold on a sec," Kim said as she rifled through her purse, extracted a hand mirror, and held it up in front of her. "There. What do you think?"

"I look like a pirate," Gin-Yung joked. A

lump of emotion formed in her throat at the sweetness of her sisters' gesture.

"A *beautiful* pirate," Chung-Hee corrected in a singsong voice. "Ginny's a *beautiful* pirate!" She began doing a little skipping dance around the ICU room while singing the phrase over and over, quietly, as if she thought only she could hear it.

"Hmmm." Kim gestured toward Gin-Yung's ears. "You know, maybe the earrings are a bit much. I'll just—"

"No." Gin-Yung brought her hands up toward her ears protectively, not wanting to change a thing about her sister's hasty makeover. "No, really, Kim. They're fine. Thank you." Gin-Yung smiled through her tears as she turned back toward the hand mirror and gazed at her reflection. *OK, Todd,* she thought confidently. *I'm ready for you now.*

As she skipped down two flights of stairs to the Dickenson Hall TV lounge Elizabeth took little comfort in the idea that she and Todd were doing the right thing by temporarily separating. Dark, persistent questions kept plaguing her— questions Elizabeth was ashamed to even think about. She shook her head vigorously to drive them out of her mind, but they kept resurfacing.

Is Todd more impressed with Gin-Yung's

unselfishness than he is with me? Does he think about me when he's with her? And then there was the darkest question of all, the one that ran continually through Elizabeth's mind, the one she felt she had absolutely no right to ask—*How long is it going to be before Todd and I can be together again?*

When she pushed her way through the door into the TV lounge, Elizabeth was determined to drive all thoughts of the day's events out of her head by spending some quality time alone with America's most reliable time-waster and mind-number. But she was surprised to see that several of her dormmates had claimed the lounge for themselves already. Nearly a dozen pajama-clad women were hanging out on the scratchy orange couches, chomping on aromatic white cheddar popcorn.

"Hey, Liz!" Carrie Levine called, waving a handful of popcorn in the air. She was dressed in pink-and-white footie pajamas, the kind Elizabeth's mom used to make the twins wear when they were seven. "Come join the slumber party!"

Elizabeth giggled in spite of herself. Everyone was wearing silly little-girl pajamas, braiding each other's hair, reading pinup and gossip magazines, and playing board games. *Maybe this evening won't be so terrible after all,* she thought, reaching for a handful of popcorn. *In fact, this could be even more of a no-brainer than watching TV.*

"Hi, Liz!" a few women shouted in unison.

"Hi," Elizabeth responded with a wave. "Looks like fun."

Jill Lombard, who lived two doors down from the twins, shoved an aluminum bowl filled with raw chocolate chip cookie dough under Elizabeth's nose. "Have some," she said, her red braids flipping in the air like Pippi Longstocking's.

"Thanks, but I'll pass." Elizabeth's stomach turned queasy at the sight of the gooey mass of dough.

Alicia Meadows, who was wearing white pajamas with big, black cow spots on them, pouted exaggeratedly at Elizabeth's overalls. "She can't join the party. She's wearing normal clothes!"

"Let's make her an honorary guest, then!" Carrie chirped.

Alicia crossed her arms mock indignantly. "It's still not fair, though. If I have to walk around looking like a cow, she should have to wear something dumb too!"

"I can go upstairs and get my flannel jammies if it will make you feel better," Elizabeth said with a sheepish laugh.

"You stay put," Carrie said in between

mouthfuls of popcorn. "I've got an idea. What do you ladies think? Should we give Liz a makeover?"

"Yeah!" the group cheered.

Carrie reached into her gym bag and took out a large plastic box. When Carrie opened the lid, Elizabeth saw that each compartment was filled with pots and compacts of wildly colored makeup. In a matter of seconds she had already spotted electric orange and pink eye shadow, blue mascara, and an assortment of glittery lip glosses. *Jessica would love this,* she thought with a laugh.

"What do you say, Liz—are you up for it?" Carrie asked.

"Of course!" Elizabeth plopped down merrily on the floor, her mood lightening considerably. It wasn't easy for her to feel sorry for herself with so many fun, vibrant people around.

"Let's see what's on the tube!" Alicia shouted from across the room. There was a sudden scuffle for the remote control, but Jill got to it first and cheered. She clicked through the channels at warp speed, from cola commercials to bad sitcoms to courtroom dramas.

Carrie dipped a makeup sponge in a pot of pale, shimmering foundation and started dabbing it all over Elizabeth's face. Leaning her head against the back of the couch, Elizabeth felt the knots in her stomach loosen. *This is perfect. I'm going to forget about everything with Gin-Yung and Todd—at least for tonight,* she decided.

But no sooner had Elizabeth begun to relax than she suddenly looked up to see the face of her ex-boyfriend, Tom Watts, up on the TV screen. Her stomach clenched up more tightly than ever.

"All right, let's watch the campus news!" Alicia shouted.

No, let's not, Elizabeth pleaded silently. She cringed, sinking into the couch cushions as if she were being swallowed up. Nothing could kill her good mood faster than having an in-your-face reason to remember the painful way her last romance had ended—especially when she was on the verge of forgetting it completely.

"In faculty news . . . Professor Felix Banks has made tenure. . . ." Tom's voice was flat and stilted as he read the news, a drastic change from his professional persona. His skin looked pasty and was drawn tight across his cheeks. His normally handsome eyes appeared sunken and tired.

Everyone else in the TV lounge seemed to notice too.

"You know, that boy could really use a makeover," Patty Sullivan drawled.

Jill giggled. "A good facial wouldn't hurt either."

Carrie, who had been rubbing a huge brush in a pot of sparkling pink blush, paused and gave Elizabeth a concerned look. "What's wrong with Tom? He looks upset."

"I really don't know," Elizabeth answered evenly. *And I really don't care either.* She glared at Tom's weary face with hardened detachment. Elizabeth could hardly feel sympathy for someone who purposely went out of his way to be cruel to her, who used every opportunity to embarrass her in front of her friends, and who took sadistic pleasure in spreading lies about her . . . even though she had once loved him deeply and unconditionally. As far as Elizabeth was concerned, Tom now deserved every little piece of misfortune that came his way. He'd certainly earned it.

Jill licked a glob of cookie dough off her thumb and pointed to the TV screen. "How come you don't read the news anymore, Liz?"

"Yeah, Liz, how come?" Carrie chimed in.

Elizabeth was startled out of her funk by the unexpected barrage of questions. "I'm taking a little vacation," she answered quickly. The truth was, she'd been having a difficult time returning to the station since her ugly breakup with Tom. Dozens of times she'd headed toward the station, ready to face him again, when suddenly her stomach would clench into a tight ball at the thought of seeing him. She'd get within inches of the doors sometimes, but to no avail. The one time she'd actually gotten up the strength to walk inside, she'd spotted Tom almost instantly and had no choice but to leave before she even got anywhere near her desk. She hadn't wanted to give Tom a reason to launch into another one of his heartless tirades.

"Well, we miss you," Suzanne Nelson said, wrapping her kitty-patterned arms around Elizabeth's shoulders.

"We sure do," Jill added. "I hope it's not for too long, Liz. You're the best reporter they've got."

Elizabeth smiled humbly. "Thanks, guys. You're sweet. Really."

"Are you going to become a journalist when you graduate?" Carrie asked as she dipped a small brush in a pot of garishly bright blue-green eye shadow.

"I'd like to," Elizabeth said, somewhat unsure of herself. Before the breakup there was nothing in the world she wanted more than to become a professional reporter, and she still wanted to. But until she could get up enough courage to face Tom on a daily basis, her dream was on hold. "Maybe someday I'll be lucky enough to work for one of the big TV networks."

Jill jumped up on the couch with a brown-and-white teddy bear tucked under one arm. "Hey, everybody, can't you picture Liz doing the nightly news?" She held an imaginary microphone in front of her and declared in a deep, professional newscaster voice, *"This is Elizabeth Wakefield, reporting from the White House."*

Elizabeth laughed wistfully, feeling the familiar hunger for news that she'd repressed for too long. *Maybe I should try to go back to the station again, for real this time,* she thought. *It would be a shame to let my dream fall by the wayside just because of a relationship gone bad. It's not my problem that Tom is acting like a jerk.* She was strong; she could handle it.

"I think you should change your name to something more *newsie* sounding, like Elizabeth Starr!" Carrie said as she put the finishing touches on Elizabeth's lip gloss with a flourish.

Elizabeth smiled unconsciously as she let her mind wander. She imagined herself standing on the Great Lawn in front of the White House; the water fountain and flowers were her backdrop. She could picture herself so clearly, as if she were on the television screen at that very moment, wrapped in a trench coat, microphone in hand, reporting some riveting piece of late-breaking, internationally significant political news. Elizabeth's stomach tingled. *I live for journalism,* she thought silently, still basking in the glow of her friends' praise. *No one, not even Tom Watts, is going to stop me from doing what I love the most.*

Chapter Seven

"Are you sure you don't want to borrow a pair of sweats or something?" Nick offered as he popped a tape into the VCR. "You don't look very comfortable."

"I'm *perfectly* comfortable," Jessica lied. She whirled around so that her elegant halter dress fluttered around her as she sat down on Nick's leather couch. "In fact, I could groove all night in these clothes," she hinted.

"Good," Nick answered, not taking the bait. "The next time we go out dancing, you'll have no problem figuring out what to wear." Dressed down in a pair of baggy gray sweats and a black T-shirt, Nick looked like he was getting ready to hibernate for the winter.

This is not *good for my social life,* Jessica thought, twirling a strand of hair around her finger.

Nick sat down beside her and propped his bare feet atop his glass coffee table. "I've been dying to see this movie," he said with a contented sigh. "There's nothing better than watching a good action flick."

Sorry, but I love being *in the action, not watching it.* Jessica rolled her blue-green eyes to the dark ceiling as the fiery opening credits began. With the tips of her delicate fingers Jessica stifled a yawn. It was going to be a long night.

Let's see what I can do to perk this evening up a bit, Jessica said to herself. Deftly she lifted Nick's arm and draped it over her shoulders, snuggling up against him. Jessica playfully tickled Nick's earlobe with the tip of her finger, trying to pull his attention away from the car chase on-screen. But Nick didn't respond. *Hmmm. Looks like I'm going to have to be a little more forceful.*

Reaching over, Jessica touched the side of Nick's face and turned his head toward her. She stared intensely into his surprised eyes, ran her hands through his thick hair, and pulled his head down toward hers. Nick's body went slack as he surrendered to Jessica's passionate kiss.

Now this *is my kind of evening,* Jessica thought blissfully. But just as Nick started nibbling on her earlobe, the phone rang.

Nick pulled his face away from hers. "Can't a guy relax around here?" he said angrily, his arms still wrapped tightly around her.

Jessica's curiosity was piqued. *Who could it be?* she wondered. Maybe the caller had some bit of news that would inject a little excitement into an otherwise painfully run-of-the-mill night. "Maybe you should pick it up," she said coolly, eyeing the cordless phone.

"Unfortunately I have no other choice." Nick sat up and grabbed the phone. "Hello?"

Jessica bit her bottom lip and watched as Nick's expression suddenly changed from a look of annoyance to one of serious concern. Turning down the volume on the TV, Jessica listened closely to what Nick was saying. Something big was brewing. She could *feel* it.

"Right, right," Nick kept saying over and over again. He took a piece of paper and a pen from the telephone stand and jotted something down. "I understand."

Craning her neck inconspicuously, Jessica tried to read Nick's notes, but she couldn't make out his scrawl. Judging from the weary lines that were forming around Nick's eyes, their movie night was about to be canceled.

"OK . . . I'll be there in fifteen minutes or so." Nick hung up the call with a beep and flung the cordless phone into the chair on the other side of the room. He let out a loud, frustrated groan as he rubbed his eyes. "All I want is some rest. Is that too much to ask?"

Jessica quickly sat upright and tucked her legs underneath her. "Who was that on the phone?" she asked innocently.

"Chief Wallace. Who else?" Nick pulled off his T-shirt, revealing the breathtaking ripples of his washboard abs. "Bill has finally been able to pinpoint the location of the biggest chop shop in the county. You should see these guys work, Jess—they're like piranhas. They can take a stolen car and strip down the parts in a matter of minutes. It's big business."

"So what's the plan?" Jessica bounced lightly in her seat, energized by the sudden change of events. She loved it when Nick talked shop—especially when he was only half dressed. He made crime fighting sound irresistibly sexy.

"We're staking out the place until tomorrow afternoon, if you can believe it. When everything's in place, we'll go in and break the operation." Nick disappeared into the bedroom and reappeared a moment later wearing a faded navy blue T-shirt and a pair of worn-out jeans with holes in all the right places.

"Where's the shop?" she asked, still admiring Nick's jeans. Jessica watched breathlessly as Nick laced up his black army boots and strapped his leather gun holster across his back.

"Down by the marina," Nick murmured absently. He tucked his badge and wallet into one of the front pockets and reached for his beat-up motorcycle jacket.

This is going to be great! Jessica thought, feeling an explosive thrill ricochet through her entire body. Undaunted by her ultrafeminine clothes, she hopped to her feet and prepared for her mission. Opening her compact, Jessica dabbed her nose with pressed powder. *Maybe I could provide the distraction while the cops move in,* she imagined, running a quick hand through her golden blond hair. With makeup and hair all in place and a spare tube of Raspberry Rendezvous lipstick in her evening bag, Jessica was ready for action.

"Let's hit the road!" she shouted, snapping her compact closed.

Nick grabbed the keys to his Camaro. "Whoa—hold everything," he said, looking at her strangely. "What are you talking about?"

"There's no way you're going to go to the marina while I sit here, bored out of my skull," Jessica said, slinging her evening bag over her shoulder. "I'm coming with you."

"No, you're not."

"Yes, I am."

"Jess—" Nick stared at her, his eyes frozen

wide in disbelief as if she'd just flown in on a spaceship from Mars and landed in the middle of his living room. "This is a dangerous sting. It's going to take at least twenty-four hours. . . . I probably won't be finished until late tomorrow night."

"But I thought this was *our time!*"

"There's no such thing as *our time* when you're dating a cop, Jessica. Remember that." He patted his jacket and jeans as if he were double-checking that he had everything he needed on him. "I'm going to have enough trouble taking care of myself without worrying about you being hurt too. You're not coming, and that's final!"

Jessica threw herself at Nick pleadingly and gripped the collar of his leather jacket firmly in her hands. "Come *on*," she whined, pouting and batting her long lashes for added effect. "You *never* let me do anything exciting."

"Is that right?" Before she knew what was happening, Nick suavely twirled Jessica around and bent her back in a graceful dip, then pressed his sensuous lips against hers in a smoldering kiss. "How's that for exciting?" he asked.

Jessica tried not to swoon in Nick's strong arms. "Real nice," she said with a throaty laugh as Nick tipped her right-side up again. "But busting car thieves might be pretty nice too."

Nick chuckled and kissed her lightly on the tip of the nose. "Enjoy the movie," he said emphatically as he turned and headed for the door.

Jessica stomped her high-heeled sandal on Nick's hardwood floor and grimaced. "*Ni*-ick—" She stopped short, realizing that she didn't really need to argue the point. As soon as Nick drove out of sight she'd just jump into her Jeep and drive to the marina herself.

"*What?*" Nick whirled around exasperatedly.

"Oh, nothing," Jessica said lightly, now dying for Nick to get out of the apartment so she could begin formulating her plan. She smiled and waved. "Have a great time, sweetie!"

A suspicious look darkened Nick's rough features. "Don't even think about it, Jess," he warned, pointing a stern finger at her.

Curses. Foiled again. Jessica rolled her eyes and plopped down on the couch, turning up the volume while Nick headed out the door. *Why does* he *get to have all the fun?* she wondered. *Life is so unfair.*

How can sick people get better in a place like this? I can hardly stand it myself, Todd thought as he neared Gin-Yung's room. There was something about the fluorescent lights, the smell of antiseptic, and the stark white hallway of the intensive care unit that seemed to drain every last drop of energy he had.

Todd put down the gift-laden bag he had been carrying so he could comb his freshly washed hair with his fingers and smooth the front of his blue cotton crew-neck sweater. Strangely, he didn't feel as if he was on his way to visit a sick friend, but more like a guy on his way to a blind date. There was so much pressure—not knowing if he would be able to overcome the awkwardness, not knowing what to expect. And it certainly didn't help that Gin-Yung had an *extremely* overprotective sister breathing down his neck.

Get it together, Wilkins, Todd coached himself silently. He took a deep breath and felt a twinge of nervousness pulsating in the pit of his stomach. *Be happy. Be confident. You've got to pour it on for Gin-Yung's sake.* Pulling his broad shoulders back and holding his head high, Todd turned on the heel of his brown dress shoes and walked toward the room.

Just as he was going to walk in, Kim bolted out of the doorway, breezing by Todd like a hurricane. "I need to talk to you for a second," she said in a low, efficient voice as she dragged him by the sleeve of his sweater out into the hall again.

Todd groaned inwardly. "What did I do wrong?" he whispered.

"Nothing . . . yet," Kim answered. She gave him the once-over and shot him a combination smile-smirk. "You're on time, you look halfway decent. . . . It's a good start."

"I've brought her a few things too," Todd said, pointing to the bag. "I told you I was going to take care of her, so you can relax, OK?"

Kim nodded, her eyes shining with reserved approval. "I know," she answered mildly. "I just wanted to thank you for really trying with Gin. Most guys your age would look the other way and run as fast as they could."

A weight seemed to lift from Todd's shoulders. "I'm hardly a pro at this."

"None of us are. We're struggling, just like you." Her face suddenly turned serious. "Gin is so happy when she sees you. That really means a lot to me. Listen, I'm sorry I was so harsh the other day—I'm only looking out for my little sister, you know?"

Todd nodded slowly. "I can respect that."

She patted the side of his arm. "You're a good guy, Todd."

"Thanks," Todd said solemnly. "You're a good sister."

Just as Kim's dark brown eyes began to well up, she quickly turned around and marched back into the hospital room with Todd trailing behind.

"Look who I found out in the hall!" Kim shouted.

"Hi, everybody," Todd said as he peeked into the room.

Mr. Suh and Gin-Yung's grandmother greeted Todd with waves and polite glances. Byung-Wah was in the corner, asleep.

"It's good to see you again," Gin-Yung's mom said warmly.

Chung-Hee dashed toward Todd with her hands raised in the air, beaming as if a movie star had suddenly arrived. The brightness of her smile made Todd look behind him to make sure that *he* was the one she was so eager to see. "I'm so glad you're here!" she shouted gleefully, looping her arm in his. "Gin-Yung's so happy to see you."

"Let me speak for myself, Chung-Hee," Gin-Yung said good-naturedly. Her smile broadened as Todd and Chung-Hee approached the bed, arm in arm. "Todd . . . I'm so happy to see you."

Gin-Yung was beaming so brightly, she almost seemed to glow from within. A soothing feeling of satisfaction quelled Todd's anxious stomach. He'd only been gone a few hours, and suddenly Gin-Yung was looking better than he'd remembered.

Is she really better, or am I just less nervous? he wondered. Somehow Todd thought it might be a little of both. A bit of color had returned to Gin-Yung's sallow cheeks, and her eyes were more clear and focused than before. A blue bandanna had been carefully wrapped around her shaved head, and a pair of gold hoops dangled from her ears. Instead of overwhelming her frail appearance, the bandanna and earrings improved on it nicely.

Todd set the packages down on the table and sat down on the chair next to the bed. "You look great," he said.

Gin-Yung touched her head self-consciously. "It was Kim's idea. I didn't have much choice but to go along with it."

"Ginny's a *beautiful* pirate!" Chung-Hee squealed, jumping in the air.

Todd laughed easily. "You're right. She is."

As if on cue, Kim rounded up her family members again and ushered them out the door. This time everyone followed without protest. "Field trip, everybody," Kim said, kicking Byung-Wah in the shin to wake him up. "Walking tour of the hospital gift shop departs from the hallway in approximately one minute."

Before leaving, Chung-Hee bounded over to Gin-Yung's bed and threw her arms around her sister's neck, planting a big kiss on her cheek. There was no timidity or fear in the little girl's face, only pure, unbridled love.

"She's an amazing kid," Todd said, holding back tears at Chung-Hee's display.

"She really is," Gin-Yung answered almost wistfully, as if she were talking about a memory. "She's going to be an amazing woman someday." Her unspoken words hung in the air between them, a pact of silent understanding. *I'll never get to see her grow up,* the silence seemed to be saying. *My younger sister will grow older than I ever will.*

A sour lump caught in Todd's throat. He reached distractedly for the packages he brought and scattered them on Gin-Yung's bed. "I brought you some chocolates," he said quickly, handing her a fancy gold foil box. "I thought you might have a craving for something sweet."

"How did you know?" she asked, her eyes wide with amazement.

Todd smiled. "Lucky guess," he answered. "Or maybe it was because I remember how you used to keep little stashes of candy all over your dorm room."

Gin-Yung's lips curled mischievously. "You never know when the late-night munchies are going to hit. A girl has to be prepared."

"Prepared? You were prepared, all right! Bags of gumdrops under your pillow, a few candy bars hidden away in between your textbooks . . ." Todd eyed the box of chocolates on Gin-Yung's lap. "If you want, I can hide the chocolates around the room so you can feel at home."

Gin-Yung was seized with a sudden fit of laughter. She held her stomach with her frail hands, tugging at the IV line attached to her right arm. Todd had almost forgotten how much he loved the sound of her laughter; it was soft and lovely like beautiful, flowing music. Tears came to his eyes once again, but he held them back. *You have to be strong,* he told himself. *You have to be strong . . . like Gin-Yung.*

"I like these chocolates right where they are, *thank you.*" Gin-Yung ran her fingertips over the ornate embossed design on the box as if she were trying to memorize every curve. Then she delicately lifted the lid and selected the very best candy in the entire box—the champagne truffle—and nibbled it slowly as though she were savoring the taste.

"Now, are you sure you can eat these?" Todd asked semiseriously. "Or are they against the rules of your diet?"

"A little chocolate sure isn't going to hurt me at this point," she said softly, handing him the box. "Have one."

Todd was about to refuse, but the earnest look in Gin-Yung's eyes convinced him to reach for a chocolate instead. His hand grazed hers as he leaned forward. Normally he would have popped the candy in his mouth and chomped on it, but at the moment it seemed rude and vulgar. Instead he placed the wafer-thin chocolate on his tongue and concentrated on the milky-sweet flavor.

"I brought you something else," Todd said, the delicious chocolate still melting in his mouth. As he handed her a shirt box tied with a red satin ribbon, a warm feeling of excitement took him by surprise. "After you returned my old basketball stuff to me last week, I thought you might want to have this." Todd rubbed his hands together, anxious to see what her reaction was going to be.

Gin-Yung untied the ribbon and lifted the top off the box. "Oh, Todd!" she said hoarsely, her mouth falling open with amazement. "I can't believe you did this!"

The light in her eyes was all the thanks he needed. "Well, you said you wanted something different to wear. . . ."

"This is so great!" Gin-Yung pulled Todd's blue-and-white SVU basketball jersey out of the box and put it on over her hospital gown. It was huge on her petite frame, the big number seventeen on the front disappearing somewhere under the blankets.

It feels like the old days, Todd thought, unable to hold back his soaring happiness. He'd forgotten how good things had been with Gin-Yung before she went away to London. *I've forgotten just how much she really meant to me,* he realized.

"Todd—" Gin-Yung's voice broke. "I can't tell you how much this means to me." Gin-Yung lay still, with her arms at her sides, tears streaming down her cheeks.

He nodded, too choked up to speak. Todd listened to Gin-Yung's shallow breaths, her lungs filling with precious air. It seemed as though he should have done something at that moment, but he didn't know what. Stiffly he reached out and laid his hand gently on her shoulder. Gin-Yung's eyes were glazed and distant. *What is she thinking about?* Todd wondered somberly. *Is she wondering how much time she has left?*

Gin-Yung pulled herself out of her thoughts and looked at the last remaining package on the bed. A smile returned to her face. "What's that?" she asked, wiping away her tears.

Clearing his throat, Todd gave her the box. "Travel Scrabble. You know, I thought it would be fun for us to play it again. If you want to."

"I'd love to!" Without a moment's hesitation Gin-Yung opened the box, her face aglow. "But as long as you don't cheat this time!"

Todd sorted through the pieces. "How can I possibly cheat at Scrabble?" he asked incredulously.

"I've seen you tuck a few extra letter tiles in your pockets."

Todd's eyes widened in mock innocence. "You never know when you might need an extra letter. A guy has to be prepared!"

The music of Gin-Yung's laughter returned. *She really does seem better than before,* Todd couldn't help thinking. *Maybe there's a chance that the doctor could've been wrong after all.* Did he dare believe that maybe she would be well again?

Gin-Yung's laughter suddenly subsided, and a look of concern spread over her face like a dark cloud obscuring the sun. "Todd, can I ask you something?"

"Sure."

"What's going on with Elizabeth? Why aren't you with her right now?"

Todd's stomach caved in. *What am I going to say?* he wondered, shaking his head and not knowing where to begin. "Elizabeth and I decided to cool things down," he said cautiously.

"Because of me?" Gin-Yung's face contorted painfully.

"Because we decided it was the best thing for both of us right now." Todd put his hand on hers reassuringly. It wasn't an outright lie, after all.

Gin-Yung squeezed Todd's fingers. "Elizabeth

is a wonderful person, Todd. Don't throw away what you have because you feel some sort of obligation to me."

"Believe me, I don't feel obligated," Todd insisted. Even though he had felt that way before, Todd was now truly speaking from his heart. "I want to be here. Right now *you're* the most important person in my life. And I'm here for you. I'm not going anywhere."

Gin-Yung's eyes misted over. "I'm so glad." She exhaled with relief. The incessant beeps of the heart monitor permeated the intensity of the moment. Gin-Yung gave Todd an exhausted smile. "We should start the game," she said lightly.

Todd balanced the miniature Scrabble board on her legs. "You go first."

Staring intently at her rack of tiles, Gin-Yung shuffled them around a bit. "You've given me some great letters." She picked up four tiles and placed them carefully on the board.

They spelled *hope*.

Chapter
Eight

"Freeze, slimeball! Drop the gun or I'll shoot!"

The sputter of a machine gun's blast riddled the million-dollar yacht with bullet holes until it looked like a sinking piece of Swiss cheese. Someone threw a hand grenade, and the hull exploded in a pyrotechnic display.

"Big deal," Jessica mumbled to the television screen. She was hardly impressed. "Nick could do that with his hands tied behind his back." Wrapped comfortably in her boyfriend's thick terry bathrobe, Jessica towel-dried her hair while she finished off the last of the action movie. Nearly an hour had passed since Nick had left for the marina—he had to be in the middle of the stakeout by now. But neither a steaming hot shower nor the handsome action hero on the television could shake Jessica out of her mind-numbing boredom.

Jessica plugged in a hair dryer near the round wall mirror in the living room. Catching sight of her reflection, Jessica sucked in her cheeks and practiced modeling. *Your time will come,* she told herself. *One day you'll be a supermodel and you'll have so much excitement, you'll have to pay people to make your life boring again.* The calendar shoot was still weeks away, but it was the only sliver of excitement she could cling to. Lifting her chin slightly and tilting her head to the side, Jessica admired her delicate, symmetrical features. *You don't need to practice,* she thought, cocking her eyebrows in approval. *You're a natural.*

The impromptu modeling session was suddenly disrupted by the ringing of the phone. *It's probably Nick,* Jessica thought, setting the hair dryer down and bounding across the room to pick up the phone. *He's changed his mind about letting me work the sting—I just know it.*

"Hello . . . ?" Jessica asked sweetly.

"Is this Jessica?"

She frowned. It wasn't Nick. "Yes, who's this?"

"Bill Fagen," the caller said. "Hey, Ronny told me you had a bulb out in your brake light. Did you get it fixed?"

"Yup. Nick took care of it for me."

"Sounds good. Say, did he leave for the stakeout yet?"

Jessica paused, her mischievous eyes darting around the empty apartment. "He's . . . in the shower," she lied. "But I can take a message for him if you want."

"Why not," Bill said. "I can trust you with important information, right?"

Jessica's spine tingled with excitement. Finally she had her chance to get involved in an under-cover sting . . . and there was nothing Nick could do to stop her. "Sure, go right ahead," she said, reaching for pen and paper.

"OK, listen carefully. Tell Nick that he's gotta bring the hubcap to the stakeout. It's really important. I'll be there tomorrow after-noon, and he really needs to have it for me then."

Jotting down the note, Jessica's brow fur-rowed at the seemingly cryptic message. "Is that all?"

"That's it. Just be sure to tell him, OK? It's crucial."

"Sure, Bill. Talk to you later." Jessica hung up the phone. *Crucial? A hubcap?* she won-dered. *How could a hubcap be* crucial? Jessica clicked off the television so she could concen-trate in complete silence. Maybe Nick needed to bring it into the shop as part of the undercover infiltration, or maybe he needed it to compare with stolen merchandise. Jessica's head swam with the possibilities. *Then again, maybe the hub-cap contains a secret homing device that will help them nab the crooks—just like in a James Bond movie!* she imagined with an excited sigh. Whatever the reason, it was obviously incredibly important.

"I *have* to find it," Jessica said aloud, her voice echoing off the apartment walls. She scoured the area, looking under the couches, opening the black doors of the entertainment center, rifling through the kitchen cupboards. "It must be around here somewhere."

She moved on to Nick's bedroom, finding nothing in the closet but clothes, shoes, and a few jackets. And a hubcap certainly wouldn't fit in one of the drawers of his bureau. Jessica sank to her knees on the green pile carpet and pulled back the bedcovers, her wet hair dripping onto the floor.

"Bingo!" Jessica shouted when she spied the shiny silver hubcap under the bed. "Well, Detective Fox, *here's* your crucial piece of equipment."

Jessica laid the hubcap gently on the couch so she wouldn't forget it, her mind humming with a rush of energy. What would she be doing wrong, after all? She couldn't leave Nick stranded in the middle of a dangerous sting without something so important. Since there was no way to get in touch with him, she couldn't exactly call and ask for his permission. And since he was going to be staking out the chop shop until the sting went down, there was no way he'd be able to come home and pick it up anyway. The only course of action left was for Jessica to go to the marina tomorrow and bring the crucial hubcap to Nick herself.

Resuming her place in front of the mirror, Jessica picked up the hair dryer and sucked in her cheeks. She turned her head from the left side to the right and back to the left again. *Modeling is so boring,* she suddenly thought. *All you do is move around a little bit and smile . . .* maybe. *There's absolutely no intellectual challenge. I mean, who wants to do something so dull?* There were dozens of more meaningful occupations out there. Like detective work, Jessica thought.

Impulsively she held her hair dryer in front of her like a gun, scrunching her face into the meanest, coldest expression she could make. "Freeze, slimeball! Drop the gun or I'll shoot!"

She examined her reflection closely. Sure, her towel-dried hair needed help, and that terry-cloth bathrobe certainly wouldn't do—but otherwise she had the look down just right. *Detective work. Yeah, that'd suit me just fine,* she thought. *Nick is really going to thank me for this.*

With a flourish she blew across the tip of the hair dryer as if it were a smoking pistol barrel. *He's finally going to see that we'll make the perfect crime-fighting team. My days of boredom are over!*

They were on the beach, walking hand in hand. The round, silver moon was directly over their heads, casting glorious moonbeams on the gently lapping waves. Todd stared up at the midnight blue sky, studded with thousands upon thousands of stars.

"It's a perfect night," Todd murmured, his voice mingling with the Pacific as it rolled against the sand. "I'm so glad you're here with me."

"Me too," Gin-Yung answered. In the glow of the moonlight Todd could see the shimmer of her long, glossy hair. Her face was healthy and beautiful, its subtle contours highlighted by a pale, muted beam.

A balmy breeze blew against Todd's face. He wanted this moment to last forever, but he knew that wouldn't be possible. Not when Gin-Yung—

"I have good news." Gin-Yung interrupted Todd's morbid thoughts and led him closer to the surf. "The doctor says I'm fine. I'm going to live. I'll make a complete recovery."

A wave crested and broke over Todd's feet, his toes sinking deep into the cool sand as Gin-Yung's words penetrated his consciousness. Their impact exploded at once, fiercely and completely, making his heart burst with joy.

"You're all right! Everything's going to be all right!" Todd laughed happily until his stomach ached. With feverish delight he wrapped his arms around Gin-Yung's waist and lifted her off her feet.

"Todd, put me down!" she screamed, playfully pounding his shoulders.

Todd spun around with Gin-Yung in his arms. The beach, the ocean, the moon, the stars, the world, the universe—everything swirled and whirled around them in a delirious, joyous frenzy until Todd spun out of control and they fell laughing onto the sand.

Gin-Yung lay back and looked up at the sky. The stars were reflected in the deepness of her eyes. "I love you, Todd," she said.

"I love you too, Gin-Yung," Todd answered, rolling onto his side. He stared down at her, awestruck by her beauty.

Leaning over, Todd's mouth found her warm lips in the dark night. He touched her cheek, feeling a crackling electricity beneath her skin. Sparks flew between their kisses. Gin-Yung was charged with life.

Out of the corner of his eye Todd spotted a figure in the distance, stretched out on the rocks. He lifted his head. Refracted moonlight shimmered and danced on the figure. It was a mermaid. In the shifting light he saw her golden hair, her full lips; her blue-green eyes burned through the night. Her fish tail was covered with jewel-like scales that glittered in the light and matched her eyes perfectly. She was watching them intently from the rock, her face distantly sad.

"You'll stay with me forever, won't you, Todd?" Gin-Yung asked, running her fingers through his hair.

"Yes. I'll be with you always," Todd said in a hoarse whisper. His eyes were still fixed on the mystical figure in the darkness. The blond mermaid moved suddenly, inching ever closer to the edge of the rocks and the dangerous plunge down to the sea below her.

"Don't go!" Todd suddenly called to the mermaid. She stopped and looked at him.

"You'll love me forever, won't you, Todd?" Gin-Yung asked.

"Yes. I'll love you always."

The mermaid suddenly moved again, her tail dangling perilously over the rocks' edge.

Todd's heart pounded in panic. "Don't go!" he called again.

She looked up at him, jewel eyes burning through to his soul. The mermaid was the most exquisite, most beautiful creature Todd had ever laid eyes on. He was suddenly afraid she would *jump, and he'd never see her again. In fact, he was almost sure of it. . . .*

"You'll never love anyone else, will you, Todd?"

"No. I'll never—"

Before the words could even fall from Todd's lips, the mermaid dove off the rocks, lost forever to the sea.

Todd watched in horror, paralyzed on the beach, pinned down by Gin-Yung's unexpectedly strong arms. "No!" he cried. "No! No!"

"No!" Todd screamed, throwing off the tangled mass of blankets that covered him. He sat up in the darkness of his room, chest heaving. A thin stream of orange light from a streetlamp streaked his ceiling.

"It was only a dream," Todd reassured himself, gasping for breath. He began to count backward from one hundred in an attempt to calm his jangled nerves. But as his terror of losing the fictional mermaid subsided, a real sense of sadness returned as he realized Gin-Yung's life was still in danger; unlike in his dream, she still hadn't made a full recovery.

How happy I was for her, Todd thought, leaning back against his pillow. *Maybe it's still possible that she could get well again.* As long as she was still alive, there was always a reason to hope.

Todd climbed out of bed and pulled off his

sweat-soaked T-shirt. He opened the window shade to let in some moonlight. The moonbeams lit his room as he grabbed a clean T-shirt from his dresser and went back to sit on his bed.

He stared out the window; it was an unusually clear night. Stars twinkled in the velvet black sky—stars that reminded him of the mermaid's jeweled eyes. *Elizabeth's eyes,* he realized. Todd stretched his arms out, as if to embrace the memory of the mermaid—*Elizabeth*—from his dream, to keep her from throwing herself off the rocks. His entire body yearned to touch her, to feel her warmth and closeness.

But the dream image of happy, healthy Gin-Yung on the beach soon crowded its way into his head once again. And with every thought of Gin-Yung that crossed his mind, the Elizabeth one faded. And whenever he fought to bring Elizabeth back into focus, he stopped thinking of Gin-Yung.

With a moan Todd dropped his hands onto his lap helplessly and started to cry. The meaning of his dream stabbed him like an icicle through his heart. *I don't want Gin-Yung to die. But if Gin-Yung lives, I can never be with Elizabeth again.*

Elizabeth marched across campus toward the TV station, determined not to back down this time. *March right in there and do your work,* she told herself, psyching herself up for a possible confrontation with Tom. *Who cares. There's nothing he can do to keep you away.* Armed with a stack of story ideas and a list of her best pieces, Elizabeth was ready for anything. Even if Tom went as far as to tell her she was no longer fit to report for WSVU, she was prepared to argue her case. *He'd be out of his mind to even try that,* she thought with pride. *He should be trying to convince me to stay.*

But deep inside her determined, empowered exterior, Elizabeth's stomach was quavering. The truth was, she'd feel much better if Tom wouldn't even be there in the first place.

You can't avoid him forever, she realized sullenly. *Even though you wish you could.* The Wednesday afternoon sun was warm on her fresh-scrubbed face, and a gentle breeze blew the soft blond wisps that loosened themselves from her professional-looking bun. *So what if Tom agrees that I should still work at the station? Then what?* It was one thing to keep doing her job, and another entirely to have to work beside someone who had absolutely no respect for her.

Do you really want to see that weasel's face every day? Elizabeth wondered as she nervously toyed with the chocolate brown print scarf she'd knotted around the collar of her crisp white blouse.

130

Sighing, she smoothed the wrinkles from her brown, knee-length skirt. *Do it for your career,* guided a little voice inside her head. *Then watch him weep like a baby when you win the Pulitzer.*

Elizabeth heaved an enormous sigh of relief as she flung open the door to the station and saw that Tom wasn't in the office. In his place Elizabeth spotted a tall guy with streaked blond, chin-length hair stacking video boxes on the shelf. Elizabeth had never seen him before.

"Hi," Elizabeth said to the guy, setting her leather backpack on one of the editing tables. "Is Tom around?"

The guy turned around smoothly in spite of the armload of videos he was carrying. From across the room Elizabeth noticed the color of his eyes—a deep, crystalline blue. She swore she saw them light up the moment they made eye contact.

"He's not feeling too well. I don't think he'll be in today." The guy set the boxes on a nearby desk and brushed his hands on the front of his olive green dress pants. The sleeves of his gray-and-white pin-striped shirt were rolled to the elbows, revealing his tanned forearms. He strolled over to where Elizabeth was standing, moving with an air of complete control and self-assurance. "Are you Elizabeth Wakefield?" he asked.

Oh no, Elizabeth thought with a hot rush of

alarm. *What other horrible things has Tom been saying about me?* She stood with the heels of her penny loafers pressed firmly against the tiled floor, prepared to defend her honor. "How did you know?"

"I'm a big fan of yours," he answered with a warm smile, extending his hand toward her. "Scott Sinclair. I just started here a couple of days ago."

"Nice to meet you, Scott," Elizabeth replied. She shook his hand hesitantly, stunned that he knew who she was and relieved that it wasn't for the wrong reasons. His hand was warm and dry. "It's always a pleasure to meet one of my fans," she said, smiling self-consciously.

Scott let out an easy, pleasant laugh. He tucked a strand of his long wavy hair behind one ear and grinned. "I've been following your stories for some time now. The piece you did on point shaving was particularly well done. You're a real pro." Scott shoved his hands into the pockets of his pants and glanced humbly at the floor. "In fact, you're the reason I'm here at WSVU."

Elizabeth pressed her fingers to her cheek to feel if she was flushing from praise. Her face was hot to the touch. *Who is this gorgeous guy?* she wondered silently. *Why is he talking to me?* Regardless of the reason Elizabeth was grateful for the diversion, not to mention the flattery. It was a nice change from wallowing in self-pity.

Elizabeth sat down on a metal work stool and crossed her legs. "You're here because of me?"

"Yeah," Scott said, pulling up a stool beside her. "See, I'm a journalist too. I write for the *Sweet Valley Gazette*. You know, I've always believed that TV journalism was basically an empty medium and that print was far superior."

Elizabeth pursed her lips demurely. "Oh, really?"

"Well, until I read one of your reports, that is," Scott said. "When I saw your work, I said to myself, 'Scott, maybe you're selling TV short. Here's a talented woman doing brilliant work on TV. It obviously can be done.'" Scott's glowing eyes stared directly at her, unblinking. "You opened a whole new world for me, Elizabeth. So I decided I had to try TV out for myself and see what it was all about."

Elizabeth shot Scott a sly, sideways glance. She was flattered, slightly offended, challenged, and curious all at the same time. "You think TV's a waste, huh?"

"Generally," Scott answered in a decisive voice. "Any true journalist knows that print is the only real kind of journalism."

"You seem very sure of yourself."

"Print is about *substance*. TV is all about image." Scott bit his lip boyishly, seemingly enjoying the sparring match that suddenly erupted between them. "I'm sure you understand what I'm talking about."

Elizabeth crossed her arms in front of her. "To a degree. I used to write for my high-school newspaper, so I understand how both sides work."

"I knew it!" Scott laughed, slapping his knee. "I knew you had to have worked in print. You're just too good to have been trained on television." When Scott leaned forward, his perfectly straight nose and full lips were only a foot away from hers. "Why did you leave print anyway?"

Hypnotized by the deep sparkle of Scott's eyes, Elizabeth had the irresistible urge to share with him absolutely everything she knew about the trade. He seemed to be hanging on her every word, eager to soak up all her knowledge. She loved the idea of being a mentor, especially with something she felt so strongly about.

"When I first came to campus, I couldn't get into Journalism I," Elizabeth admitted, almost apologetically. "I didn't want to give up working on the news, but I didn't have a lot of options. Then Professor Sedder suggested I try out for WSVU. So I did, and, well, here I am. But I do have to admit that the glamour of working for television was a bit of the allure."

"And was it as glamorous as you thought?"

"It was a lot more *work* than I thought!" A flood of memories overcame Elizabeth as she was reminded of those first few weeks of working with Tom. *We clicked so well*, she remembered with a touch of sentimentality. They'd shared the same vision and the same drive—Elizabeth had never met anyone as dedicated to journalism as she was. *Who knew that inside the sweet, wonderful man I loved lurked the heart of a beast?*

Elizabeth snapped herself out of her trance. "There was always editing and splicing that had to be done, voice-overs, copy to write."

"So you worked on other people's pieces?"

"We have to," Elizabeth said, suddenly feeling like an expert. "There's a small staff—if we want to get out the broadcast every night, we have to share the responsibility."

Scott nodded slowly, but it wasn't in agreement—it was more like he was planning his next argument. "It's too bad that you have to do other people's work."

"There's nothing wrong with a collaborative effort. It's one of the best ways to learn," Elizabeth countered.

"Point well taken." A dreamy expression flitted across Scott's handsome face. Elizabeth had the impression that he was an idealist and his beliefs were positively unshakable. Scott's eyes narrowed. "But don't you miss the freedom of

135

having a piece that is entirely your own, without having to be involved in other people's work? Don't you miss being able to craft a story solely on your own words and not having to worry that the copy matches the images you have on video? Don't you miss the pride of seeing your name in print, alone in the byline?"

"Television allows for a different kind of creativity."

"I'm sure you know better than I do."

Without thinking, Elizabeth reached out and touched Scott's forearm. "You'll understand better once you've worked here for a while. I'll show you the ropes."

Scott's lips parted in a gleaming smile. "Thanks, Elizabeth. I look forward to it," he said, standing up. "But right now I'm starving. Before we get to work, how about we grab a bite to eat?"

"Let me see. . . ." Elizabeth glanced around the office. *What if Tom finds out I came in to work—and immediately left for lunch with a gorgeous intern?* The thought of facing Tom at all, for even one second, made her suddenly shudder with revulsion. *Who cares? I don't have any work to do here anyway.* With determination Elizabeth grabbed her backpack and slid off the stool. "OK. Let's go."

Chapter
Nine

"OK, Tombo," Danny Wyatt said as he cracked open his logic book. "What is a syllogism?"

Tom slumped in his library seat and stared numbly at his roommate. "I don't care."

"Wrong answer!" Danny cheered, doing his best game-show host imitation in the middle of the reference section. "The correct answer is, 'Two statements from which a conclusion follows necessarily. For example: All dogs are animals; all animals are mortal; therefore all dogs are mortal.'"

"Whatever," Tom said sullenly. He appreciated his roommate's attempts at helping him study, but he just wasn't in the mood to play along. Tom didn't think he'd ever care about anything if he couldn't have Elizabeth back again.

Danny's handsome brow wrinkled with concern. "Come on, man. You have a logic test tomorrow. You've got to get your mind off the bad stuff, at least until the test is over. You've got to focus."

"Thanks for the pep rally," Tom said dryly, resting his chin on his hands. "But Hawkins can fail me if he wants to. It doesn't matter."

"So you're just going to let everything fall apart around you without doing anything about it?"

"That's the plan," Tom muttered.

Shaking his head, Danny slammed the book shut. "I thought I'd never live to see the day when Tom Watts turned into a coward."

Tom suddenly sat up. "What was that again?"

"You heard me," Danny answered, looking slightly pleased with himself for getting a rise out of him. "I said you were a coward."

"I am *not* a coward."

"You could've fooled me."

"Look, it took a lot of courage for me to talk to you about this whole thing, Wyatt," Tom said, pointing at Danny for emphasis. "It was hard for me to realize that I made a big mistake by not trusting Elizabeth. But I did. That proves I'm not a coward."

Danny folded his muscular arms and leaned back in his chair. "But the only person you've admitted it to is *me*. If you *weren't* a coward, you would've told Elizabeth . . . and Dana too."

"I'll tell them as soon as I can, Danny. I just found out, so give me a break."

"I think you knew deep down that you were wrong a long time ago," Danny said bluntly. "At least, maybe you hoped you were wrong."

Tom leaned forward, throwing himself fully into the good-natured sparring match. "Is that so? What else do you think, all-knowing one? I'm dying to hear your psychic insights."

"We-ell, since you asked . . ." Danny flashed his friend a sly smirk. "I also think you couldn't admit that things weren't clicking with Dana, so you copped out and led her to believe that you two had a future together. Coward once again, my friend."

"Hey! I'm no coward. I honestly like Dana, and she knows that. She's a great person," Tom argued. He quickly scanned the stacks to see if anyone was eavesdropping on the conversation, but luckily they were in the middle of the lunchtime lull and there were very few students around. "And I *wasn't* leading her on, Nostradamus. I just didn't know what I wanted, that's all."

"Yes, you did. You wanted Elizabeth, right?" Danny's mouth drooped in a dour expression. "Don't lie to me, buddy."

"Y-Yes . . . and no," Tom stammered, suddenly feeling as if he were being interrogated by an FBI agent. "I mean, I wanted her the way she was before, not when I thought she was lying to me."

"And why did you think she was lying to you?"

Tom's head began to throb. He knew that Danny was only trying to make the situation clearer for him, but Tom was beginning to regret ever coming to his roommate for advice. "I thought she was lying because I didn't think my father was capable of the things she'd accused him of."

"Wrong." Danny leaned forward on his elbows and stared at Tom from across the table. "You believed Elizabeth was lying because you weren't willing to face your father, get to the bottom of the situation, and find out the truth for yourself." A self-satisfied smirk twisted his lips. "Therefore you are a coward."

"Well, at least one of us is going to pass his logic exam tomorrow," Tom said wryly. Opening his notebook to a blank page, he began drawing aimless circles with a ballpoint pen. "Instead of just making me more confused, how about using some of your logic to help me out of this mess?"

Danny's face softened. "You're a smart guy,

Tombo. I thought you would've figured it out yourself by now. Just tell Elizabeth you're sorry."

Frustration boiled inside Tom's stomach as if it were a smoldering cauldron. All Tom seemed to be able to do was stir his emotions around and around in helpless circles when what he really needed was to find a way to put the fire out. "How can I make it up to Elizabeth after all the horrible things I've done to her?" Tom cried. "How can I tell her how sorry I am and how much I miss her? How can I tell her that having a family means practically nothing to me now? How can I ask her for forgiveness?"

Danny patted Tom supportively on the shoulder. "You just did, man. You couldn't have said it any better. You should go see her this afternoon and tell her everything you just told me."

But Tom knew deep down that that wouldn't be as easy as it sounded. The pained look Tom had seen in Elizabeth's soft blue-green eyes every time he had been mean to her was permanently etched in his memory. He felt as if he were drowning in guilt.

"I can't say these things to her face, Danny. I'm too ashamed of how I've treated her," Tom said. "Besides, she's with Todd Wilkins again. I should probably just leave her alone."

"You at least owe her an apology," Danny

answered. "Write her a letter. Write down everything you said to me and give it to her."

Tom sighed, his chest crushing under the weight of his anxiety. Danny did have a good point: At the very least, Elizabeth deserved an apology. Then why was he so terrified to do it?

Maybe Danny's right, he thought apprehensively. *I* am *a coward.*

"OK. I'll write the letter," Tom blurted, anxious to erase any cowardly notions from his mind. "But I can't deliver it to her in person."

"Why don't you leave it on her desk at WSVU? That way you'll know she gets it." Danny collected his books and tossed them into his gray canvas backpack. "I've got to get going—I'm meeting Isabella for lunch."

Tom watched his roommate with admiration as he zipped up his backpack. "Thanks for the advice. Really."

"My pleasure, Tombo. I enjoy giving you a hard time." Danny grinned. "Later."

"Wait," Tom pleaded when he remembered whom Danny was meeting. "Please don't tell Izzy about this. I don't want anyone to talk to Liz about this whole mess before I have a chance."

"You have my word . . . on one condition."

"What's that?"

"Write the letter now before you lose your

nerve."

Tom nodded and gave his best friend a sheepish grin. "I know. That sort of thing happens all the time when you're a coward like me."

"No," Anthony said as he impatiently tapped out a rhythm with his conductor's baton. "You're coming in too late. Try it again."

Dana positioned her fingers carefully on the neck of the cello and listened to the beats Anthony was counting out. On the fourth count she drew the bow across the strings, filling the air with a low, sonorous note.

Anthony sighed and slapped the baton on the edge of the music stand. His cheeks were blotchy and red. "Come on, Dana. You were half a beat too late again. This is one of the easiest passages in the entire piece."

"I'm sorry." Dana wiped her perspiring forehead with the back of her hand. She squinted at the sheet music in front of her, but for some reason she couldn't seem to visualize how it was all supposed to come together. For the moment the notes had lost all meaning to her; they just looked like a series of lines and dots.

Anthony pushed back his short, dark brown hair in frustration. He looked as if he was about to blow his stack any second. "I just don't get it. You were playing so perfectly the other day. I thought we'd be able to go on to the next movement by now."

"I'm having an off day, OK?" Dana snapped. "Why can't you cut me a little slack?"

"All right, all right, I'm sorry," Anthony answered calmly, holding his hands up in surrender. "Why don't we take five and you can tell me what's eating you."

Carefully resting the cello on her stand, Dana followed Anthony out of the practice room and into the hallway. An eclectic blend of sounds seeped out of the various rooms and mingled inharmoniously in the hallway: a trumpet ran through a series of arpeggios, a piano played ragtime, a bass guitar resonated with a bluesy thud. Dana couldn't help but think that the chaotic music was the perfect accompaniment to the tangled web of emotions trapped inside her.

Anthony handed Dana a paper cup filled with water from the cooler at the end of the hall. She sipped it slowly and took a seat on the padded bench.

"So what is it?" Anthony asked as he sat down beside her. "What's killing your concentration?"

Dana frowned. She didn't want to tell him the truth. The last thing in the world she wanted to hear right now was *I told you so*.

"It's Tom, isn't it?" Anthony guessed, right on the money as usual.

Dana drained the last of her water and crushed the paper cup in her fist. "You know when we walked to the parking lot together after my last lesson? Within five minutes after you left, he told me he needed some time alone." Her stomach ached as she remembered how lost and distant Tom seemed. "He said he didn't know what he wanted."

Anthony's eyes widened. "I thought you two had just spent an incredible weekend together."

"We did." Dana exhaled loudly, somewhat comforted that Anthony was finding the situation just as strange as she did. "But he's making me start to wonder if it was all in my head . . . if there was ever anything between us to begin with."

Leaning casually against the back of the bench, Anthony took a drink of water and stared at the framed time line of the history of opera hanging on the opposite wall. Instead of just saying, "I told you so," he seemed to be taking her plight very seriously.

Dana waited patiently for Anthony's advice. Her music professor was one of the wisest, most perceptive people she knew. Whatever Anthony advised her to do, she'd do. He wouldn't steer her wrong.

Finally after several minutes he spoke. "And

you say you were totally surprised by this?"

Dana nodded furiously. "I was shocked. I still am."

"But didn't you tell me that he was still in love with his ex-girlfriend?" Anthony probed.

Elizabeth. The mere thought of her name drained every last drop of energy Dana had. How could someone Dana hardly knew have so much control over her life? Sure, Tom was still in love with Elizabeth—it was no secret. But from what Dana understood, the circumstances surrounding their breakup were far too emotionally charged; their relationship had exploded into tiny bits and had absolutely no hope of being repaired. Other than Tom being a little distracted now and then, Dana had never seen it as an insurmountable obstacle.

Until now.

"A lot of guys are still hung up on their former girlfriends," Dana argued. "They learn to get over it."

"But Tom hasn't."

Dana's hazel eyes dropped to the orange-and-yellow speckled carpet. "So what do I do now?"

"Convince him that you're the one he wants to be with, not Elizabeth," Anthony suggested. "Didn't you say that when you put your mind to something, you're unstoppable?"

"I know, I know. But he's so *distant*. I'm not

even sure he wants me around."

"But Tom said himself that he doesn't know what he wants," Anthony said. "So it's up to you to help him decide."

Dana suppressed a surge of hope that was burning in her chest. Could she really convince Tom that they were meant to be together?

Anthony tossed his empty paper cup in the wastebasket. "Tell me something, Dana. Do you love this guy?"

Dana nodded slowly. "I think I really do."

"Then *fight* for him," Anthony said. "Use all the passion you put into your music to play the game of love."

Dana seized her professor's words and held them close to her heart. It made perfect sense. Tom was too confused to really know what he wanted; just because he had said that it was over between them didn't necessarily make it so. Maybe it was just moodiness that had made Tom say those things. Or maybe he had simply been too impulsive. Whatever the case, Dana was convinced that if she threw all her determination and energy into getting Tom back, he would finally give up on Elizabeth.

"Thanks, Anthony," Dana said with a grateful smile. The tension in her body subsided.

"No problem," he answered, getting to his feet. "But I'm afraid my reasons are purely selfish. I want you to get your love life straightened out so you can start hitting those notes again."

Dana laughed. "Don't worry. I'll have my focus back very soon." As she followed Anthony back to the practice room, the wheels of her mind started spinning wildly as she began plotting her scheme to get Tom back. *Step number one,* she calculated silently, *get rid of Elizabeth Wakefield.*

"As soon as Dub gives us the signal, we'll load up the van," Bill Fagen said as he anxiously paced the concrete floor of the abandoned warehouse. "How're you feeling, Nick? In good shape?"

"I'm all right," Nick said coolly. He sipped a cup of strong, black coffee to keep alert and tried to ignore the tingling anxiety that trickled up and down his spine.

In the long hours since he'd taken the call from Chief Wallace, he hadn't been able to make it home. He'd suffered through a dull, uneventful night of staking out the chop shop next door, and his body ached from the quick nap he had taken at his desk back at the precinct at the break of dawn. Worst of all, he hadn't had a chance to talk to Jessica since he'd left her at his apartment, and he'd had no messages waiting for him at the station or on his home machine.

But now, in the course of the past hour, Nick had finally moved past feeling exhausted. His body was fueled by coffee and pure adrenaline.

Bill stealthily slid over to one of the soot-covered windows and peered out, careful not to be seen. "How many men do you think they've got waiting for us?"

Nick tossed his empty paper coffee cup into a rusty oil barrel. "We've only seen about five guys entering the place this morning. Mechanics, mostly. Unless they have a secret entrance we don't know about, there shouldn't be any surprises."

"Don't count on it," Bill said, strapping an extra clip to his holster. "There are always surprises."

"You have the backup squad on alert, right?" Nick asked. "As it is now, our men are one-to-one with theirs, but if something unexpected happens . . ."

"Don't worry," Bill said, sliding away from the window. "We can handle those creeps."

Nick walked over to the light blue van in which he and his crew were going to be hauled, Trojan horse style, into the chop shop. He opened the side door and looked inside. Nick and Bill and a few of the other guys were going to be hiding in the van while Dub Harrison, the undercover cop who had made a deal with the crooks, was going to drive the van right into their shop. Then, at the precise moment—*boom!* They were going to throw open the door and burst out like an army battalion. It was their riskiest infiltration yet.

I wish we were going in there right now, Nick thought as he reached for one of the spare revolvers on the floor of the van. His fingers were trembling slightly, either from coffee or from nerves—he couldn't be sure which.

The toughest part of Nick's job, he felt, was waiting for something to happen. When Nick was in the middle of a sting, there was no time to think, only to react. His instincts took over, giving him complete concentration and control over every movement. But when Nick was waiting, there was time to second-guess, to worry, to be afraid. And in his business fear was deadly.

"Where's Dub?" Nick asked. He loaded the gun and strapped it to his back, the seconds ticking down like an eternity.

"Soon," Bill replied, running his hands through his hair. The wait seemed to be getting to him too. "Dub will be here real soon."

Nick sat down on the floor of the van. The deafening silence of the warehouse was eating at his already raw nerves. "I picked up your hubcap," he remarked in a lame attempt to make light conversation.

"Yeah, thanks." Bill's eyes widened as if he'd completely forgotten about it. "Can I have it?"

The corner of Nick's mouth turned up in a smirk. "It's all yours, pal."

"No, I mean, can I have it *now*, smart guy."

"What? Did you think I'd bring it to the *stakeout?*"

Bill scratched the top of his head. "Well, yeah, since I asked you to. Didn't your girlfriend give you the message last night?"

Uh-oh. Nick's heart dropped with a sickening thud. "What message?" he asked wearily.

"I called your place last night and I talked to Jessica," Bill said. "She said you were in the shower, but that she'd pass along the info as soon as you got out. Didn't you get the message?"

In the shower? Nick wondered. *I didn't even have a chance to take a shower last night.* Suddenly it all clicked into place.

"Oh, I got the message all right," Nick said ruefully. His stomach clenched into a tight ball of worry as he wondered what sort of crazy scheme his girlfriend was cooking up.

I never should've opened my stupid mouth about the sting, he told himself, a shiver of fear prickling the back of his neck. *"Down by the marina."*

What a sap. I'm an idiot, the way I let her charm information out of me. Silently Nick prayed that Jessica would have at least enough common sense to stay far away from the operation. Otherwise she would be putting all their lives at risk.

Chapter
Ten

"This is *so* exciting!" Jessica could barely contain herself as she sped her Jeep through the narrow streets near the marina. The silver hubcap occupied the bucket seat next to her, wrapped protectively in a blanket. Jessica reached across the seat and touched it often. The crucial piece of equipment was her ticket to a career as a police detective.

Nick is going to flip when he sees me, Jessica thought, taking a sharp curve to the left. *He thinks I'm just playing around about being a detective, but I'm dead serious.* So serious, in fact, that Jessica had done painstaking research to make sure her appearance at the stakeout was absolutely perfect. Her investigation consisted of watching several action movies from Nick's video collection and taking careful notes of what the female crime fighters in each movie were wearing. Cross-referencing the information with the contents of her closet, Jessica came up with an outfit that could turn any hardened criminal into a quivering puddle of jelly—sleek black leggings, a black, scoop-neck bodysuit, and sexy leather knee boots.

Whizzing by the mildewed wooden docks, Jessica spotted the warehouse one block ahead. The Jeep's tires squealed as she pulled into the nearest side street and parallel-parked behind a suspicious-looking delivery truck. Cutting the engine, Jessica quickly reached for the hubcap and took out the most important element of her disguise—a sophisticated pair of Italian designer sunglasses.

Scope the area first, Jessica told herself as she stepped out of the cherry red Jeep. Pulling the shades down to the tip of her nose, Jessica scanned the narrow alley for potential suspects and other unsavory characters. The street was absolutely empty—unusual for a Wednesday afternoon. *Maybe the sting is already going down,* she reasoned, pushing her sunglasses back into position. Jessica's heart pounded fiercely against her rib cage.

It was show time.

Holding the hubcap tightly under her arm, Jessica skipped across the cracked pavement toward the warehouse, careful not to scuff her boots on any loose stones. The building was a large, gray, rectangular structure with huge garage doors on the side of the warehouse that faced the water. There were no windows on the first floor and only a few grungy panes on the second. Shiny new cars lined the side of the street closest to the warehouse, but still there wasn't a soul in sight.

Jessica was surprised to find she was actually getting a little nervous. *Where's Nick and the rest of the guys?* she wondered. *Are they inside already?* An icy shudder moved down her back. *What if my delivery puts these guys in danger?* The question crossed her mind for a split second before the answer came to her. *Nick will probably be in more danger if you don't get the hubcap to him,* she reasoned. If things turned bad, then she'd just have to be the one to save the day.

With her keen detective's eye Jessica made a quick appraisal of the warehouse. The garage doors were closed, and she certainly couldn't stroll in through the side doors—she might ruin the sting. There was only one way into the building, and it was *up*.

A welcome burst of adrenaline flooded Jessica's body as she reached for the rusty fire escape ladder hanging above her. Firmly grabbing the rung with her free hand, she made a mental note to buy a pair of leather gloves for her next stakeout—she couldn't risk ruining her professional manicure even if it was for the noble cause of fighting crime. Jessica pulled the ladder down and began her unsteady climb to the second floor. The air caught in her throat as she scaled the rickety ladder, never looking down but focusing her eyes on the dirty window above. The thin edges of the hubcap bit into Jessica's side as she held it tight against her body.

Hang on, Nick. I'm almost there.

Reaching the top of the tiny fire escape, Jessica gently tugged at the sash and the window opened noiselessly. She breathed a heavy sigh of relief, knowing that soon she would be off the rusty fire escape and safely on the second floor of the warehouse.

But what awaited her inside the building was much more treacherous and horrifying than Jessica could have ever imagined. There was no second floor at all—instead there were open rafters, a complex network of steel beams and a narrow wooden catwalk from one end to the other. From there it was a straight drop to the cement floor fifty feet below.

This is just like in the movies! Jessica thought with glee as she carefully crawled through the window onto the shaky wooden catwalk. The boards gave slightly under her weight. A rush of heady excitement flooded her senses as she peered over the makeshift pipe railing and gazed down at the scene unfolding below. Five guys wearing greasy jeans and T-shirts gathered around a light blue van and started taking apart the vehicle piece by piece. They didn't speak to one another, yet everyone seemed to know exactly what needed to be done and what they were each responsible for. The mechanics were young, around Jessica's age, and the entire operation was overseen by a burly, shady-looking man who was dressed in a three-piece suit. He stood off to the side near what appeared to be an office, smoking a cigarette and sneering menacingly at the workers.

Where's Nick and the other detectives? Am I at the wrong place? Jessica gripped the thin railing and closed her eyes for a moment, feeling a little woozy from the height. She could hang loose for a few minutes until Nick arrived—if he was going to arrive at all—but what if one of the mechanics spotted her in the rafters? Jessica swallowed hard at the idea. There was no one to protect her, and the only weapons she had at her disposal were her to-die-for good looks and a flimsy old hubcap.

As determined as Jessica was to help bust the criminals, she knew she couldn't do it alone.

Carefully she walked backward toward the window, the dry crackle of wood sounding with each step. *Easy does it, Jess,* she told herself. Tiny beads of sweat trickled down her brow. *Careful, you're almost there. . . .*

Suddenly there was an explosion of shouts erupting from below. Startled, Jessica reeled backward against the window frame, steadying herself by reaching for the nearby railing of a narrow wooden staircase that led to the ground floor. She looked down and watched as the doors of the pale blue van whipped open and the undercover cops jumped out. Nick was the first one out, gun poised for action, looking incredibly cute in his black leather jacket.

"Put your hands up!" Nick shouted, waving his service revolver at the stunned men. The other detectives formed a semicircle near him and secured the rest of the area.

"Up against the wall—now move it!" Nick barked.

That's my boyfriend! Jessica thought with pride, nearly melting at the tough way Nick clenched his jaw. The stunned mechanics scurried to the wall like frightened mice and did whatever Nick told them to do. They raised their arms in surrender while the undercover officers patted them down for weapons.

Jessica had started down the perilously steep

wooden stairway to join the guys on the floor when something caught her eye. She looked up to see the burly man in the dark suit hunkering down in the dark little side office—somehow he had escaped the roundup. Nick and the rest of the guys were too busy reading the mechanics their rights and snapping on handcuffs to notice the man with the shifty eyes moving into position from the darkened doorway.

Jessica's heart stopped. She stood there, on the wooden steps, gripping the handrail with her sweaty fingers, looking at Nick and the officers, then back at the creepy man again. Clearly the detectives had no idea the guy was hiding out there. If they didn't see him soon, there was a good possibility that he would get away, and the entire case would be shot.

Just as Jessica was about to call the suspect to the officers' attention the man stepped out of the office, carrying a black semiautomatic weapon. The snub-nosed barrel of the gun was aimed directly at Nick's head.

"Please hurry! I can't take it anymore!" Gin-Yung shrieked in agony.

The needle was a welcome sight. Gin-Yung clenched her jaw and closed her eyes as she waited for the nurse to inject her arm with the only fluid that could dull the roaring pain raging through her body. But each shot was less effective than the last. It was taking longer and longer for the painkillers to take effect, and they seemed to be wearing off sooner every time.

Gin-Yung watched as the syringe was emptied into her vein, but nothing seemed to be happening. The fire still raged on. *It will be soon. Hang on just a little longer . . .*, Gin-Yung told herself, gritting her teeth against the pain. Kim sat beside her, holding her hand. Gin-Yung squeezed her sister's fingers so hard, she thought they might break. Was the pain actually giving her some kind of bizarre strength? *Hang on. You can do it. One . . . two . . . three . . . four . . .*

"It's not working!" Gin-Yung cried in anguish to the nurse. "Please . . . please give me something else!"

The nurse pressed two fingers against Gin-Yung's wrist and took her pulse. "Give it just a few more seconds."

"It's not working! I know it's not!" Gin-Yung sobbed uncontrollably, hoping she'd black out rather than endure one more moment of excruciating agony.

Mr. Suh stood up and ushered little Chung-Hee out of the room. "Please! Get something else!" he shouted to the nurse. "My daughter's in pain!"

The nurse's face paled. "I'll see what I can

do," she answered as she shuffled out of the room.

"Hurry!" Kim called after the nurse, her eyes wet with tears. She turned back to look in Gin-Yung's face. A tear fell on her bedsheet. "Hang on, Gin. She's coming right back."

A mild numbing finally set in. It was just enough to take the edge off, but it still left Gin-Yung feeling violently nauseous. *When is this going to be over?* she wondered as her face and body became consumed with tingling heat. Silver spots swam before her eyes, and she could feel her throat begin to constrict and release involuntarily. Clutching at her stomach, Gin-Yung leaned over the side of the bed and began to gag.

Kim rushed to grab a pail and held it steadily under Gin-Yung's head as she got sick. This wasn't the first time it had happened, and Kim seemed to have grown accustomed to her duty. When she was done, Gin-Yung threw her throbbing head back on her pillow, sweat and tears streaming down her face.

"My poor, sweet child," Mrs. Suh cooed as she soothed her with a cool, damp washcloth while her father took the pail out of the room. Byung-Wah poured a glass of water and offered it silently, his mouth tense around the edges. Gin-Yung sipped lightly while her mother held the glass for her.

161

Suddenly Gin-Yung burst into tears at the indignity of it all. She felt like a helpless infant, unable to control her body or her emotions. It was no way to live.

Kim stroked her sister's damp forehead. "You're going to be all right, Gin."

"No . . . I'm not," Gin-Yung answered listlessly. Her lungs felt as if there were leaden weights pressing down on them. "It'll only get worse. . . . I don't want . . . to live anymore . . . not like this."

"Oh no, Gin," Kim whispered, darting her eyes over toward the rest of the family as if she wanted to make sure they hadn't overheard her morbid statement. "Please don't say that."

The nurse reappeared and injected Gin-Yung with a second needle, this one taking effect almost immediately. Gin-Yung eased her head against the pillow, still holding her sister's hand. A wave of relief moved over her like sun-warmed ocean water, lapping and flowing, gently bringing her back to a more tranquil state. Her head felt heavy, as if it were filling with the warm, sweet water.

Kim laid her head on the pillow beside her sister. "How is it now?"

"Better . . . ," Gin-Yung moaned. The sluggish gray water returned, filling her eyes and ears, enveloping her.

Kim cried softly, warm tears falling onto the pillow. She held her hand against her mouth, her shoulders shaking.

"Don't . . . Kim . . . ," Gin-Yung whispered. "So tired . . . don't want . . . to live like this."

Mrs. Suh buried her head in the blankets and sobbed. Brave, silent tears coursed down Byung-Wah's cheeks. Gin-Yung heard their cries, saw their tears, but she was floating too far away to feel their pain.

"I love you, Gin," Kim cried, resting her cheek against her sister's shoulder. "I'm going to miss you so much."

"My family," Gin-Yung whispered as she fell deep under the waves and closed her eyes. "So beautiful. Can't . . . say . . . good-bye."

"Imagine I'm a prominent member of the faculty," Elizabeth told Scott as they stretched out on the grassy quad for lunch. "Imagine I've been at SVU for five years, have published two important books, and have been actively involved in student affairs, but the university denies me tenure." Elizabeth popped the cap of her raspberry iced tea and leaned back against the trunk of the nearest tree. "Go ahead—interview me."

Scott unwrapped his smoked turkey sandwich, his brow furrowing in thought. The bright California sun lit his blond hair with streaks of copper and gold. "Professor Wakefield," he began, holding an imaginary microphone in his fist. "Could you please explain to everyone why you believe you were denied a promotion?"

Elizabeth shook her head furiously and waved her hands in the air. "Hold it right there," she said, halting the mock interview. "That question would never work for TV."

The corners of Scott's mouth drooped. "Why not? It's a direct question that would be on all the viewers' minds."

"It's too in-depth," Elizabeth argued. She nibbled at the corner of her tuna salad on wheat, relishing every moment of their discussion. Teaching Scott about television journalism was the perfect way for her to push her troubles out of her mind—at least for a while. And she certainly couldn't have asked for a more attractive and attentive student.

"Too *in-depth?*" Scott asked incredulously. "You must be joking."

"You've got to go for the sound bite," Elizabeth continued. "The small phrase that reveals everything. Ask a question that the subject can answer in one concise statement, not a long-winded speech."

Scott groaned loudly. "See what I mean?

Why just serve nuggets of information when you can really get to the bottom of a subject?" He rolled his crystal blue eyes skyward. "It seems so pointless. If you're going to cover a story, do it right—or don't do it at all."

The muscles in Elizabeth's neck tensed and her face burned with the sting of Scott's barb. Did he think of her as a second-rate journalist just because she put her energy into the campus station instead of the paper? "Television doesn't work that way," she answered defensively, her voice rising in pitch. "There are time constraints in a broadcast, you know. News has to be more direct and concise. You have to work *with* the medium."

"Elizabeth." Scott's eyes were warm and kind as he smiled apologetically. "Please realize that I'm not criticizing *you*—just television. That's all. I certainly didn't mean to imply that you were stupid for doing broadcasts. I was just comparing the differences between the two media. All the work I've seen you do has been terrific—the best. Really."

"Well, thanks, Scott," Elizabeth answered with a humble nod, the tension in her muscles dissolving. Even though she could feel her defenses falling away, she still blushed a deep crimson. "I realize we don't have to agree, but I do confess I was getting a little offended."

Elizabeth took a tiny, self-conscious bite from her sandwich and concentrated on the golden highlights in Scott's hair; his eyes were too intense to meet.

"Sometimes I just don't know when to shut my big mouth. I'm sorry if I ticked you off." Scott looked shyly at the ground and twisted tender green blades of grass in his fingers. "You know, when I was doing some filing the other day, I came across your clips."

Elizabeth was so surprised, she nearly choked on her sandwich. "What?"

Scott continued to look down, plucking grass compulsively until there was a round, bald patch of lawn near his foot. "I didn't snoop around too much. I just couldn't resist reading your old print articles. They were phenomenal."

"Th-Thanks. I don't know what to say," Elizabeth stammered, flustered by his praise. "I'm proud of those pieces. I—I really worked hard back then."

"It shows. Now, please don't be offended when I ask you this," Scott said cautiously, fixing her with a handsomely earnest gaze. "But I'm just curious . . . why are you wasting your talent on *fast-food* journalism? You were obviously born to write. You belong in print."

"And if I'd had my way when I came to SVU, I would have *stayed* in print," Elizabeth remarked, her eyes meeting Scott's penetrating stare. "To be honest, I miss it a lot. It was a challenge . . . even more of a challenge than having a conversation with you."

Scott laughed. "I'll take that as a compliment."

"You should!" Elizabeth exclaimed. "I mean, talking to you has really made me remember what it's like on the other side. And I haven't been challenged like that in ages. It feels good."

Scott nodded solemnly, his lips curving into a brilliant smile. "It feels good to me too."

Chapter Eleven

"Come on, coward. Don't you dare lose your nerve," Tom muttered under his breath as he descended the stately front steps of the library. With his letter of apology to Elizabeth gripped firmly in hand, he headed toward the campus television station, knees trembling with apprehension. "You can do this. Be tough."

I hope Elizabeth's not around. Tom's darting eyes traced a quick triangle from the library to the clock tower to the coffeehouse; Elizabeth was nowhere in sight. The knotted muscles in his shoulders loosened with relief. *I can't see her—not yet,* he thought. *Not until she's read the letter. Not until she knows how sorry I am.* Tom knew he wouldn't be able to handle seeing a look of disgust on Elizabeth's fragile face, smoldering hatred in her beautiful eyes.

Especially since he knew he deserved every bit of it.

Tom continued on down the path. Drops of sweat rolled down the middle of his back, making him shiver. His pace slowed as he neared the WSVU building, the glass doors of the studio seeming strangely ominous in the afternoon sun. This was it. Soon Elizabeth would know how devastated Tom was for all the wrongs he had done her and how desperately he wanted to make them right. After she read his letter, there would be no question in her mind as to how deeply he still loved her. *But does she still love me?* he asked himself. *Am I too late to win her back?*

Tom was suddenly struck with paralyzing fear. After Elizabeth read the letter, what would happen next? What would she say? Would she say anything to him at all? Or would she ignore his apology—and him—completely, just to make him suffer? *Even though I deserve it, I couldn't bear being ignored by her,* he realized. *But I couldn't bear knowing that she didn't love me anymore either.* Anxiety drilled through Tom's torso. *The only thing I could bear knowing would be that she still loved me. And that seems to be the least likely result of them all.*

A sudden nervous clench shot through Tom's stomach, and he doubled over, sucking in a sharp breath. He managed to slump down on the nearest wooden bench, the precious envelope still clasped in his damp fingers.

I can't go through with this. Tom broke into a cold sweat. There was no way Elizabeth would forgive him for all the horrible things he had done—Tom couldn't even forgive himself. He already knew what she would say; there was no point in setting himself up for the inevitable agony of rejection.

I hate you, Tom Watts. He could imagine her clear, musical voice spitting out those words. *I hate you forever for what you've done.*

He'd be hard-pressed to put it better himself.

"You might as well cut your losses, Watts," Tom grumbled as he clutched his aching sides. "You'll never get her back."

On the other end of the bench Tom spotted a wastebasket. He slid over and held the letter above it, ready to let it drop into the pile of trash. But something held him back.

You never know, his conscience told him. *Elizabeth is a forgiving person. Maybe she'll find it in her heart to give you another chance.* Tom grasped the envelope firmly and took a deep breath. *Besides, she deserves an apology from you even if you don't win her back.*

Before he could change his mind again, Tom hopped off the bench and ran into the building.

Luckily the station was empty. Tom strolled

over to Elizabeth's narrow metal desk and traced the edge of it with his fingertip. Nostalgia swelled in Tom's chest as he glanced at the paperwork Elizabeth had sorted into neat piles and the flowered mug she always kept filled with razor-sharp pencils. He knew Elizabeth couldn't stay away from the station much longer. Journalism was her life.

Tom set the letter on the top of Elizabeth's in-box, carefully arranging it so it would grab her attention. *I've done everything I can do,* Tom thought sadly as he headed toward the door. *The rest is up to you, Elizabeth. Our future is in your hands.*

The thief had the barrel of his gun trained directly at the back of Nick's head, and his pudgy finger was poised on the trigger. Jessica's heart thundered in her chest as she watched the horror unfold right before her eyes. As the thug slowly crept up behind her boyfriend Jessica's mind whirled around frantically. *Don't just stand there,* a voice inside her head screamed. *Do something!*

That's when she remembered the hubcap. It all happened in an instant—a quick aim, a flick of the wrist, and the silver disk was airborne, sailing toward the thief like a huge, metallic Frisbee. Jessica waited in breathless anticipation, hoping to knock the man out cold, but the flying hubcap floated gracefully over everyone's heads, completely unnoticed, until it smashed against a wall and came crashing down in the corner of the warehouse.

Clang!

Everyone, including the fat little man with the gun, looked around to see where the noise was coming from. Jessica took the split-second diversion as the perfect opportunity to send out a warning. "Nick!" she yelled, her voice echoing off the concrete walls. "Watch out!"

Nick spied Jessica on her perch high above the floor. Jessica motioned for him to turn around and Nick reacted quickly, spinning on his heel. No sooner did he see the crook coming at him with the gun than Nick shot the weapon out of the man's hand. The other cops jumped on the assailant and flattened him to the ground.

"Oh, Nick!" Jessica yelped joyfully as she descended the rickety stairs to the ground floor. "I'm so glad you're OK!"

Nick shoved his service revolver into his holster and wiped the sweat off his brow. "Jessica," he hissed, his deep green eyes ablaze, "what are you doing here? You could have gotten yourself—not to mention everyone else here—killed!"

Dub Harrison, fellow undercover cop and champion wisecracker, sized up Jessica with an amusing sneer. "Had to bring your girlfriend along, huh, Fox?"

"Shut up," Nick snapped, his laser-beam eyes still on Jessica.

"I just didn't want to be left out," Jessica pouted. She struck an alluring pose, hoping Nick would get a load of her sexy new leather boots. "I deserve some excitement too, you know. Why should you be the one to have all the fun?"

"Fun?" Nick stared at her incredulously. "This isn't *fun*. It's *work!*"

Just as Jessica was about to argue her case, the door to the back room burst open and two men came out, shooting wildly around the chop shop. Nick grabbed Jessica by the shoulder and pushed them both to the floor, guiding her to safety behind a partially dismantled pickup truck.

Nick was seething. "I can't *believe* you came here," he said, teeth clenched.

"Excuse *me* for trying to do you a favor," Jessica retorted.

Gunfire exploded from all sides. Even though the bullets were whizzing dangerously close to her head, Jessica couldn't help but think of how romantic it was to be held in the protective arms of a gorgeous undercover cop during a risky sting operation. It was pure, unadulterated, shaking-in-your-leather-knee-boots excitement. Just like in the movies.

"Stay here," Nick said forcefully, the veins near his temples almost bursting. He drew his gun. "Did you hear me, Jess? *Stay put* until I tell you it's safe to come out."

Jessica ducked down behind the back tire. "All right, Nick. I've got *the point.*"

"I can never be sure with you." Stretching out flat on his belly, Nick crawled along the cement floor like a snake, squirming out toward the gunfire. Jessica watched as his torso, then his legs, and finally his sneakers disappeared around to the front of the truck. Jessica hunkered down as low as she could with her back against the truck's wheel, hugging her knees to her chest. *Go get 'em, Nick,* she silently cheered. *Show those car choppers who's boss.*

Then a sharp whistle split the air. Jessica couldn't see what was making the noise, but it sounded like a bottle rocket. Seconds later the missile hit its target—the windshield of the truck Jessica was hiding behind—and there was an enormous explosion of glass.

"Nick!" Jessica screeched, covering her head with her hands as pellets of shattered glass rained down around her. After the sharp burst of noise trailed off, the room fell strangely silent.

Jessica brushed off the crumbled safety glass and peered under the truck to try to see what was going on. Nick seemed to be OK—he seemed to have made it around to the other side of the truck before the windshield exploded. He continued to slither along stealthily, then suddenly he stopped short.

Squinting, Jessica poking her head under the truck's intricate exhaust system to get a closer look. All she could see were the cuffs of a pair of stylish black pin-striped pants and a pair of feet comfortably nestled in expensive shiny dress shoes. The shoes walked over to where Nick was lying down and stopped an inch from his face.

"Nick . . . Nick, what's happening?" Jessica hissed across the floor. Nick didn't answer. His eyes rolled upward, toward some object that was out of Jessica's view.

Jessica slid herself farther under the truck. Straining to see, she rolled over onto her back and looked up. The owner of the shoes leaned over and grabbed Nick roughly by the shirt and dragged him up to his knees. Then he put the barrel of his gun against the side of Nick's head.

The look of fright in Nick's eyes made Jessica bite down on her lower lip to keep from screaming. Nick dropped his gun, too far out of Jessica's reach, and held his hands up in the air.

The man in the pinstripes reached down and dragged Nick up to his feet.

"Tell your buddies to drop their guns too!" a gruff voice demanded. "I'm not going back to jail! There's no way I'm going back there!"

"Take it easy, man," Nick said in a low, even voice. "Just take it easy."

This seemed to rile the crook even more. "I mean it! Tell them to drop their guns or it's all over for you, buddy."

Jessica rolled out from underneath the truck and hid behind the nearest wheel. She was Nick's only hope now—but what on earth was she going to do?

"I had such a good time at lunch, Elizabeth. It's hard to go back to work," Scott said as he held open one of WSVU's glass doors for her.

Elizabeth flicked on the overhead lights and sighed. "I know exactly what you mean." Her eyes fell on one of the station's many video cameras, perched on its rolling tripod in the corner of the room. The editing equipment was lined against the back wall, silent. There had been a time when just looking at the studio equipment filled Elizabeth with a warm bubble of inspiration. But now she felt empty and cold. The same old things just didn't excite her anymore.

Elizabeth tossed her backpack lazily on the

conference table. "I have absolutely no desire to work with any of this stuff today."

"Was it something I said?" Scott asked, his mouth twisting into a boyish grin.

"It was *a lot* of things you said," Elizabeth admitted. "I mean, why am I really here anyway? It's not the glamour—I'm hardly the glamorous type. And while a larger audience is nice, it isn't nearly as important as getting to the truth."

Scott beamed brightly, sitting down on a stool. "I'm glad to see that some of the things I said didn't go unheard."

"I heard every single word," Elizabeth replied.

Brushing a strand of blond hair out of his eyes, Scott gazed at her intently. "Tom must be so happy to have you on board. You're really the driving force behind this place."

Looking away, Elizabeth paced the station floor pensively. Before, she'd resisted talking about Tom, but now she found herself wanting to open up to Scott—at least a little bit. "Let's just say that Tom's enthusiasm has cooled off considerably."

"How so?"

"I don't really want to get into it," Elizabeth said quickly, suddenly regretting she'd said anything. "We had a sort of falling out."

A grave expression overshadowed Scott's features, and the corners of his mouth tightened. "I'm so sorry to hear that," Scott said simply, not pressing for more information. It was as if he understood not only what Elizabeth said but what she *didn't* say as well.

"It's all right," Elizabeth murmured, smiling faintly.

Scott reached out and held Elizabeth's hands in his. It was an oddly intimate gesture, something she would've expected more from a close friend and not from someone she'd met only an hour or so ago. Yet somehow it felt right at the moment. Elizabeth allowed herself the luxury of feeling the warmth of his hands and staring deeply into Scott's mesmerizing, jewel-like eyes.

"Elizabeth, I don't know what happened between you and Tom—that's your business. But it really bothers me to think that you're spending your energy in a place where your talent is unappreciated."

He had a point. *Why should I work so hard for someone who doesn't trust me? Why should I put all my energy into making a creep like Tom Watts look good?*

Scott continued on, still holding her hands. "Sometimes when a journalist stays in one place for too long, stagnation sets in. It's important to breathe life into your work by exposing yourself to a new, more invigorating experience—so you don't fall into a rut."

"Is that what you think has happened to Tom?"

"I can't really say," Scott said hesitantly. "All I know is that I decided to strike out and give WSVU a chance—you know, to try something different. But the attitudes and the way things work . . . well, it's just not for me."

"Sorry," Elizabeth deadpanned. "I guess I didn't do a good enough job of showing you the ropes."

Scott laughed. "Funny you should say that. It's not really your presentation that's the problem, Elizabeth. But somehow I get the feeling that you're not too hot on remaining here yourself."

Elizabeth looked down at the floor and flushed. *I guess I can't hide my true feelings,* she realized. *Maybe it really is true—perhaps I just don't want to work here anymore.*

"Now, I know that you and I are different people," Scott continued, "but maybe it's time you moved on and tried something different too. All it can do is help you grow as a journalist."

Elizabeth pulled away from him and smiled coyly. "If I didn't know better, Scott, I'd think you were trying to get me to quit my job here."

Scott ran his hands self-consciously through his hair and looked around as if he suddenly felt like he was intruding. "I apologize. I was only trying to help you out a little," he said innocently. "I certainly didn't mean to cause any trouble."

"You didn't cause any trouble at all," Elizabeth answered with a smile and a dismissive wave. "In fact, I'm glad we had this talk. You're a good salesman, Scott. And you know what? I'm starting to think that maybe I would like to try my hand at print again."

The tension in Scott's brow eased. "That's— that's great."

"But don't think you can take the credit for this," Elizabeth warned good-naturedly. "My boyfr—a very good friend of mine gave me the idea not too long ago."

Her heart gave a quick twinge when she remembered how Todd had suggested she leave WSVU the previous week. *I haven't thought about Todd for hours,* she realized. *I'm glad I ran into Scott—there's nothing like good, intellectual conversation to keep your mind off your troubles.*

"You should really give it a try," Scott said, jolting her from her thoughts. "I guarantee that if you go to work for the *Gazette,* your talents will not go unappreciated."

Elizabeth let out a deep breath and smiled.

Scott's enthusiasm was like a spark; it seemed to reignite her passion for journalism. She certainly couldn't argue with his logic. She *had* grown too comfortable at the station, too complacent. And now that her relationship with Tom had dissolved in cruelty and mistrust, the tie that had been binding Elizabeth to WSVU only seemed like a flimsy, useless thread. *It's time to be stimulated, to stir things up a bit,* Elizabeth decided. *I'm ready for a change.*

"So . . . what should we do now?" Scott asked, getting to his feet. "Should we stick around and finish up some work here? Or perhaps I could introduce you to a few people at the *Gazette*. The senior editor raves about your work. . . ."

Elizabeth remained silent as second thoughts began creeping into her brain. *Should I really leave for good?* she wondered. It all seemed so final.

Wistfully she looked around the station. On the shelves stood stacks of black video boxes, each containing hours and hours of footage she and Tom had taped on location together. The saggy old couch against the back wall—the one with the springs jutting out of the cushions—was where they used to take kissing breaks during the many marathon editing sessions that had lasted into the wee hours of the morning.

Hanging high up on the wall was the old, too reliable clock, with its round white face and schoolhouse numbers. They lived by that merciless clock as it quietly, dispassionately counted down the seconds from one deadline to the next.

Oh, Tom, why did you throw it all away? Elizabeth swallowed hard, feeling a hard lump of nostalgia rising in her throat. There was no doubt in Elizabeth's mind that she'd miss the excitement of television and of being with Tom, but things were different now.

Yes. It was time to move on.

"I think we should go," Elizabeth said quickly, clearing her throat. Her blue-green eyes filled as she made a fleeting tour of her desk. There were a lot of things she wanted to take with her—her flowered mug, the pieces she'd been working on, photographs and clippings she'd saved. Through the blur of her sentimental tears she could even see that there was a stack of mail sitting in her in-box, including an envelope that appeared to have her name handwritten on it in bold letters. Despite her curiosity Elizabeth couldn't handle sticking around one more minute longer. "Let's get out of here, Scott. I can pick up my stuff later."

Scott nodded enthusiastically and grabbed

his books. "You'll see how great this change will be for you," he said. "Get ready for the best career move you've ever made."

"Terrific." Elizabeth slung her leather backpack over one shoulder; her eyes were burning, but the tears never fell. "When can I start?"

"I'll kill you! I swear!" shouted Phil "The Chopper" Wuxtry, the chop shop's dangerous ringleader. "Tell them to drop their guns!"

Nick gagged as Wuxtry pulled him into a tight, painful headlock, his arms falling limply at his sides in surrender. Wuxtry's gun was hard and cold against the back of his head as he heard the ominous *click* of the safety being released. Yet none of this scared Nick nearly as much as knowing that Jessica was around, a loose cannon just waiting to make some stupid move that would get her—and everyone else within a ten-mile range—killed.

"You heard him, guys," Nick choked. "Drop your weapons."

One by one Nick saw the agents carefully place their revolvers on the floor, moving slowly and deliberately so as not to put Nick's life any more in danger than it already was.

Nick looked out of the corner of his eye to try to see where Jessica was, but he couldn't spot her. His focus and concentration were dissolving rapidly, replaced instead by a paralyzing fear.

"Back up against the wall!" Wuxtry shouted as he tore the key chain from the belt loop of Nick's jeans. With his gun still trained directly at his head, the well-dressed crook backed over to where the handcuffed mechanics were and released one. After Wuxtry handed the keys off to the freed mechanic, he stalked back over to where Nick stood and resumed holding him in his tight, strangling grasp.

"Everybody stay calm." Nick's voice wavered, betraying the hard expression that was fixed on his face. "We can work this out."

"We're going to work this out, all right," Wuxtry answered menacingly. "As soon as we free our men we're going to tie all you cops together, bring you out to the docks, and give you a group swimming lesson."

And what will happen to Jessica? For some reason the thugs hadn't looked for her yet. But it wouldn't be long before they did. Nick's heart thundered in his ears. The musty smell of rusted metal filled his nostrils with each quick intake of breath. One by one empty sets of handcuffs clinked to the floor.

The fifth set of handcuffs was tossed. "Cuff 'em," Wuxtry growled. "Smitty, get some rope."

The freed mechanics picked up the cuffs and began restraining the cops.

"Hey, boss, what about the girl?" one of them said.

Nick tried to squirm out of Wuxtry's grasp, his chest feeling as if it were collapsing on itself.

"Oh, yes . . . the girl," the ringleader said. "Find her and bring her over here. I have a special treat for her."

You'll have to kill me first! Nick tried to jab his elbow into Wuxtry's side, but it was to no avail.

"I hope you cops know a thing or two about synchronized swimming." Wuxtry cackled uncontrollably with Nick still locked under his arm. "You're going to need it."

Suddenly Nick heard a hollow *thunk* and felt a heavy shudder pass through his captor's body. As if in slow motion Nick turned to see Wuxtry's eyes roll up in his head as he let go of Nick and silently crumpled to the floor.

Stunned, Nick turned around and caught Jessica's little shrug as she stood there, sheepishly holding an enormous wrench she had obviously used to knock the crook out cold. In a fraction of a second, before anyone had time to react, Nick grabbed the semiautomatic weapon out of Wuxtry's hand and swept it across the chop shop.

"Freeze!" Nick shouted roughly, his strength—and pride—returning.

"Yeah! Freeze, slimeballs!" Jessica chimed in. "Drop the rope or my boyfriend will shoot!"

"Jessica, please!" Nick hissed under his breath. But he couldn't believe his eyes when he saw the mechanics put their hands up in the air and stare at Jessica in outright fear.

Bill and Dub, who hadn't been handcuffed yet, grabbed their guns and tackled the few remaining suspects who had made a break for the back door. In the blink of an eye the situation was once again under police control and the thieves were in custody.

Nick wiped his dripping forehead with his sleeve and leaned weakly against the side of the truck, taking in slow, deep breaths. Never in a million years did he think they'd be able to turn that situation around—especially not with everyone intact.

Sauntering over to him, Jessica beamed proudly. Nick met her glowing smile with a cold, hard stare.

Jessica's eyebrows arched in stunned surprise. "What's the matter?"

"I can't *believe* you came here when I *specifically* told you not to," Nick said through gritted teeth.

"But I *had* to come, Nick," Jessica answered

defensively. "I had to bring the hubcap. Bill made it sound so important."

Nick glanced over at the mangled metal disk lying on the floor in the corner. "Hey, Bill. Your hubcap is here," Nick shouted with a jerk of his head.

"I know," Bill answered mournfully.

Nick smoothed back his dark, tousled hair and glared at Jessica with an uncharacteristic fury smoldering in his green eyes. "I'm not even going to *ask* what your warped little mind thought it was for, but the hubcap belongs on Bill's vintage Thunderbird. I picked it up for him as a favor." He looked away from the dented hubcap, his expression turning even more sour. "It was extremely rare, and I'm not so sure he's going to be able to find another one."

Jessica's heart sank. "Well . . . maybe we can get it repaired or something. I mean, what's the big deal? It's just a piece of—"

"Go home," Nick answered in a chilling voice as he turned to join the rest of the cops who were loading the thieves into the powder blue van. Part of him wanted to hold Jessica close, to tell her how relieved he was that she wasn't hurt. But the fury that boiled inside Nick made him keep her at arm's length. "We'll talk about this later."

"Wait!" Jessica desperately called, clinging to

187

Nick's arm as she tried to crawl into the van with him. "Didn't we do good?"

"Good?" Nick answered incredulously, shaking Jessica off. "This was a *disaster!*" He motioned for Jessica to back away from the van, and the moment she was at a safe distance, Nick slammed the door in her face.

Chapter
Twelve

"What happened?"

Todd's words evaporated into the stagnant hospital air as he ran gasping into the waiting room. Kim had called him at his dorm room just minutes before, saying only that he should get there as fast as possible. Without even giving it a second thought, Todd grabbed his car keys and raced to the hospital.

It can't be that bad, he'd assured himself on the drive over. *Gin-Yung looked great the last time I saw her.*

But as he stood in the entrance to the waiting room, Todd's hopes sank like a lead balloon. Mr. Suh was wandering around the room in a daze. Mrs. Suh was stony and silent, her face contorted. The scene made Todd's legs threaten to give way beneath him. The news had to be bad.

Please . . . please don't let me be too late, Todd prayed silently, reaching for the nearest chair to steady himself. *Please, please, please give me one more chance to see her. Let me at least have a chance to say good-bye.* Deep sorrow coursed through every fiber of his being.

Kim suddenly spotted Todd and motioned for him to come sit next to her on the couch. Todd slowly made his way across the grim waiting room, his reluctant feet dragging behind him like weights. He stopped right next to Kim, who reached out and touched his hand.

"You got here fast," she said, her voice shaken.

"Is she still . . . here?" Todd muttered urgently. He hoped Kim understood his vague question. He just couldn't bring himself to ask, point-blank, *Is she dead?*

Kim nodded slowly. "She's taken a bad turn, Todd. The doctor says that she doesn't have much time left."

Gin-Yung is still with us, Todd thought gratefully. *At least I'll have a chance to spend more time with her.* He gave Kim's hand a squeeze and exhaled, enjoying a brief moment of relief before the full impact of Kim's words hit him.

She's taken a bad turn . . . she doesn't have much time left. . . .

Todd felt the blood rush from his face. "I—I don't get it." He stared at Kim uncomprehendingly. "Gin-Yung was doing fine yesterday—"

"It was very sudden. Dr. Madison already told us that drastic changes are common. We should have expected it." Kim let go of Todd's hands and broke down crying.

Gently he put his arm around her. "If drastic changes are so common, maybe she'll get better again. Maybe this is just a temporary setback," he said delicately.

Kim lifted her head and looked up at him. Her hair was stringy, pasted to her wet, puffy cheeks. "Gin-Yung's not going to get better, Todd," Kim said in a flat voice. "Even *she* knows it."

Todd reeled from the crushing blow of Kim's words, feeling as if he'd just been kicked in the stomach. "Is she conscious? Can I see her?" he asked numbly.

"She fades in and out," Kim said tiredly, wiping her tearstained cheeks with the palms of her hands. "You can visit, but the doctor won't let you stay very long. Go see her, Todd. She needs you."

Todd felt numb, as if he had just been jolted by an electric shock, paralyzing his thoughts and his body. In a thick, murky haze he headed toward the ICU wing like a zombie, his feet carrying him clumsily, woodenly.

The trip down the stark, misty hallway seemed to last an eternity. When Todd finally arrived at room number six, he found Gin-Yung propped up in bed with pillows around her, staring blankly off into the distance, as if she could see through the hospital walls. Gin-Yung's skin was grayish white and dark circles surrounded her sunken eyes. Todd felt his stomach clench fiercely for a second time as his own eyes confirmed what Kim had told him.

She must be so scared, Todd thought, desperately wishing he could take some of her burden upon himself. He walked in, and the empty sound of his dress shoes scuffling on the floor seemed to rouse Gin-Yung slightly. She acknowledged him with a smile so faint, Todd thought he might have imagined it.

"How are you feeling?" he whispered, sitting on the edge of Gin-Yung's bed. He reached out and held her hand, startled at how cold it was to the touch.

"Been . . . better . . . ," Gin-Yung said, slowly forming the words in between tired gulps of air and harsh gasps. Her eyes were glassy, focusing not quite on Todd but somewhere just beyond his right shoulder.

I can't believe she can still joke around at a time like this. She's so brave. Todd forced a relaxed smile on his face, trying to hide behind his fright. Her translucent skin and protruding cheekbones haunted him.

Gin-Yung seemed to be withering away right before Todd's eyes.

"Can I get anything for you?" Todd asked, looking around for something—*anything*—that could make her more comfortable. "Is there something you want?"

"Won't be . . . long . . . now," Gin-Yung muttered throatily, as if she didn't hear him. "I can . . . feel . . . it."

Please don't go, Todd begged silently. *Not yet.* Something suddenly cracked inside him, breaking wide open like a water dam bursting under too much pressure. It left him with a raw, gaping wound that stung mercilessly.

"Do you have any idea how much I'm going to miss you? How much we're all going to miss you?" Todd heaved deep, anguished sobs and buried his face in the blankets on her bed. Gin-Yung moved her hand slightly, touching the side of Todd's face with the tips of her fingers.

The nurse popped her head in the doorway. "Excuse me, Mr. Wilkins, I'm afraid you'll have to leave. Gin-Yung is very excitable. She needs her rest."

Just as Todd was about to sit up, he felt Gin-Yung's open hand pressing gently against his head, as if she was trying to keep him right beside her. Her touch was gentle but unequivocal in its meaning.

In Todd's mind the gesture summed up Gin-Yung's spirit perfectly—tender in demeanor, yet unquestionably strong at the same time. As he felt her fingers graze his cheek the wound in his heart lost some of its sting. *Yes, Gin-Yung,* he thought. *I will stay here for you. I will do anything for you.*

Todd reached up and gave Gin-Yung's frail hand a reassuring squeeze before he raised his head and faced the nurse. "I'm going to stay," he said firmly.

A look of distress flashed in the nurse's eyes. "You may come back in two hours, Mr. Wilkins. But for now I insist that you go back to the waiting room."

"I won't," Todd declared, bolstered by the energy flowing through Gin-Yung's delicate hand. "I'm not leaving her."

The nurse's lips pinched together tightly. "Please don't force me to call security."

"Do whatever you have to do," Todd challenged mildly. "I'm not leaving."

"Fine," the nurse growled before she turned on her heel and walked out of the room.

"We did it." Todd bit his lower lip and smiled. "We did it, Gin."

"Thanks," Gin-Yung whispered.

Todd stared deeply into Gin-Yung's dark, tear-filled eyes, searching to connect to the woman he had known before. And she wasn't difficult to find—not as difficult as Todd might have imagined. Down beneath the agony and the suffering, underneath the frail body that had betrayed her, beyond the sadness and the disease, she was there. She'd always been there.

Aching to hold her, Todd laid his head against Gin-Yung's rib cage, his arms on either side of her. Closing his eyes, Todd pictured the vibrant, fun, beautiful woman he had once loved and then had let fall by the wayside. The one he had just now rediscovered.

Yes, I did love you, Gin, he thought, his eyes stinging as he remembered how only days ago they'd insisted that they'd never really loved each other. But now, after finding out that Gin-Yung had lied about having a boyfriend so that Todd wouldn't feel guilty about dating Elizabeth, he knew she'd been lying. And he knew he'd been wrong. *We really were in love, Gin. I know it must have hurt you to lie like that. And I was so wrong to believe you.*

Todd felt Gin-Yung's cold fingers trace his hairline, as if she knew what he was thinking and was trying to put a stop to it. He looked up to see that her eyelids bobbed heavily and her head rocked slowly from side to side. "Sing . . ." Her

195

voice trailed off into a series of wracking coughs.

"It's OK, Gin," Todd said, rushing to get her a glass of water. She shook her head slightly when he brought it, as if she knew it wouldn't do her any good.

"Sing . . ."

"Sing?" Todd was frightened. Was Gin-Yung talking some kind of nonsense? Was she about to—*no. Gin-Yung is not going to die. Not yet. Not now.*

"Sing . . . me . . ."

"Yes?"

Gin-Yung's face relaxed into a beatific smile. "Sleep."

Sing . . . me . . . sleep. "Sing you to sleep?" Todd asked, his eyes refilling with tears when he saw her nod imperceptibly. His whole body shivered, and his soul was crushed by the sweet, innocent tenderness of her request.

"You mean, like a lullaby?" Todd cleared his throat. "That's . . . that's a pretty tall order, Gin." He laughed nervously, but Gin-Yung kept smiling.

Deeply, sonorously Todd began to hum a nameless lullaby as he entwined his fingers in hers. He could almost feel the vibrations of his throat resonating throughout her frail body. Soon he began to sing out loud, at first softly and meekly, then with confidence and emotion as Gin-Yung began to drift off into peaceful sleep, her smile never leaving her face.

My baby, Todd thought, treasuring each second that dangled between them like a priceless, irreplaceable jewel. *My sweet, sweet girl. I will never forget you, Gin-Yung.*

"Where is everybody?" Dana said aloud as she walked into the WSVU office early Thursday morning. The overhead lights were off, all the equipment was down, and the blinds were closed. She didn't see anyone except for the security guard at the door.

According to Tom, Thursdays were usually the busiest days of the week at the station. Even if no one else felt like showing up, Dana knew that Tom the workhorse was always there putting the finishing touches on a story or starting a brand-new one. So why wasn't he around this morning?

I bet it has something to do with Elizabeth Wakefield, Dana thought ruefully, hitching up her black leather jeans by the belt loops. She could just picture Tom moping in his room, mooning over Elizabeth, too depressed to get out of bed. Or maybe he was sitting under Elizabeth's window, throwing pebbles against the pane until she looked out to see what was going on.

Elizabeth, Elizabeth, Elizabeth . . . I bet that's all Tom ever thinks about. Dana sighed. Tom was obviously so blinded by misguided love that he couldn't even see his *true* perfect match when she was staring him in the face.

"I'm starting to wonder if you're worth the trouble, Tom Watts," Dana said to the empty room as she twirled a curly strand of mahogany hair around an index finger. The heels of her motorcycle boots scraped lazily against the floor as she slowly walked the perimeter of the room.

Of course he's worth it, she told herself silently. Tom was one of the most intelligent, intense, and passionate men she'd ever known. So what if he was hard to get? The game of cat and mouse they were playing was turning out to be a very challenging one with each passing minute.

"So what do I do now? Wait until the little mouse shows up?" Dana plopped down on Tom's desk chair and stared at the sea of paperwork that covered every inch of its surface. Did he have an appointment book, a calendar—anything that might give a clue to his whereabouts? Dana lifted stack after stack of paper and pile after pile of videocassettes, but she found nothing.

"OK. I guess I really gotta get my hands dirty." After stealing a quick glance at the door to make sure no one was watching her, Dana began snooping through the drawers of Tom's desk, enjoying a delicious thrill at the possibility of uncovering any one of Tom's deep, dark secrets. All she came up with were boxes of staples and pens, neatly organized file folders, and a miniature plastic football.

"You are *so* squeaky clean, I can't stand it." Dana groaned as she slammed the last drawer closed. Flustered, she swiveled the chair around and came face-to-face with a gigantic calendar hanging on the wall behind Tom's desk. "Oh, there you are," she deadpanned. "I've been looking all over for you."

Dana zoomed her finger over the calendar's surface and poked the proper Thursday. A tiny twinge of discovery traveled up her spine when she noticed that Tom had scrawled something in the box, but it was quickly squelched when she realized that his handwriting was completely illegible.

"Log . . . logi . . . login. Login . . . exit. Login exit." Dana paused and tilted her head to the side for a moment before throwing up her hands in surrender. "I give up. I mean, what the *h-e*-double-hockey-sticks is a *login exit* anyway?"

She jumped out of Tom's desk chair and paced his office. The only thing left to do was to come back later, or maybe drop by Tom's room unexpectedly. *Or maybe I should just follow Elizabeth around*, she thought wickedly. Wherever she was, Tom couldn't be too far behind.

"Well, since I'm already here. . . ." Dana sauntered over to Elizabeth's desk. How could she resist the overpowering urge to snoop through it, to find out every detail about her life? She surely couldn't be as perfect as she seemed—there had to be some explosive secret that was just waiting to blow up in Elizabeth's face. And Dana wouldn't mind being the one to expose it if it meant getting Tom's full attention.

Dana scanned the nauseatingly neat surface of the desk. Nothing there. She flipped through a few files, looked for secret compartments . . . still nothing. "Another squeaky clean one," she muttered dejectedly. "How depressing."

Just as she was about to open the top drawer, an envelope lying on top of her in-box caught her eye. *Elizabeth* was written in the same bold, scratchy handwriting that Dana had seen on the calendar. As much as the thought repulsed her, the letter had to be from Tom.

Dana's pulse quickened as she looked around again, but no one was in sight. Without a moment's hesitation Dana snatched the letter out of the box and opened it, pacing around the room as she read.

*   *   *

Elizabeth—

I know I'm probably the last person you want to hear from right now, but I need to tell you two things.

You were right about my father.

I'm sorry.

I'm so sorry, Elizabeth. I'm so sorry for everything I've put you through. I would gladly give it all up if I could just go back in time and erase what I've done.

I really would do anything for you. I wasn't willing to when you came to me with your secret, but I was blind. I didn't know how blind until I realized how much I missed you.

My life has been meaningless without you. Not even having a family has been able to fill this dark emptiness inside me. Nothing interests me, nothing excites me. My desires and goals have evaporated. I've been walking around like an empty shell, with nothing to fulfill me or sustain me except the memory of you— when you still loved me.

Your laughter rings in my ears. Sometimes when I close my eyes, I can still smell the warm, soft scent of your hair and taste the sweetness of your lips.

My memories of you are the only rays of light I have to lead me through the darkness.

I know that forgiveness is too much to ask for, but I have to take that chance. I love you—I've never stopped loving you. I'm begging you, Elizabeth, please let me make it up to you. Please say yes and give me my life back.

Tom

Dana stood frozen in the middle of the room, her hand clamped over her mouth in horror. Each agonizing word left a painful imprint on her heart. So it was true—Tom was still madly obsessed with Elizabeth.

What about me, Tom? Dana wanted to cry. *When have you ever cared about me?*

The envelope was burning in Dana's palm. She couldn't return it now that it had been ripped open. *Why would you even want to return it in the first place?* questioned a tiny voice inside her head. *It's fate—Elizabeth is never supposed to see this letter. You and Tom are meant to be together.* There was no arguing with fate.

Calmly she replaced the letter in its envelope, folded it in half, and stuck it in the back pocket of her leather jeans. With a casual yet purposeful stride she headed for the station's front doors.

Just before she reached them, the security guard smiled and nodded politely at her. "Did you find what you were looking for, miss?"

"Sure did," Dana answered brusquely.

Chapter
Thirteen

So peaceful here. I never want to leave. Don't make me . . . I'm not ready.

Gin-Yung felt her body rising to the surface of consciousness. It was morning. She'd made it through another night. Her eyelids rolled back from her eyes, letting in shards of light. She woke to a hazy, silent room, colors spinning and rolling amid the cool, dark waves.

"Good morning," she heard a quiet voice sing, then a light, whisper touch danced across her cheek.

"Kim?" Gin-Yung rolled her head to the side to see a blurred yet angelic face hovering near her. It seemed almost otherworldly.

"No, it's me, Todd. Kim and your family are in the waiting room." The angel's voice was hushed and warbled, as if he were talking underwater. His face came closer, its handsome features washing in and out of focus. "They'll only let two people in here at a time to see you now. I wasn't supposed to stay the whole night, but they couldn't drag me away from you."

Gin-Yung couldn't smile, even though she wanted to. She stared up at the angel through the cocoon of water that encased her, his face shimmering in the waves. "Not . . . scared," she murmured, the air whistling in and out of her lungs. Gin-Yung paused. The effort it took to speak seemed to strain nearly every muscle in her body. "Ready."

Her fingers were pressed to something soft— a pair of lips. "You're so brave, Gin. The bravest person I've ever known."

Gin-Yung's eyes rolled upward and caught a gray shadow on the ceiling before darkness passed over them.

"I don't know if I could be so strong," she heard a deep voice say. A strong hand stroked her cheek gently.

"You," Gin-Yung replied weakly, the light coming back again in dim bursts. "Love."

The angel leaned over her and stared deeply into her eyes. His loving gaze penetrated the murky waters surrounding her body. "Only when I'm with you."

A wave took her, buoying her body up, then

down in the current, first hot, then cool. Gin-Yung was letting go, letting her body be taken, not fighting against the wave. "Angel," she gasped breathlessly, searching for his face in the shifting light. "Todd."

"What?" the voice came again. "What is it, Gin?"

"Kiss . . ." A wheezing breath shook her body. "One . . . last . . . time . . ."

Water drops fell on her face. "It won't be the last, Gin. I promise."

Soft, warm lips pressed against hers. Love and tenderness pulsed through her body as Gin-Yung melted into the indescribable sweetness of the kiss. She closed her eyes, losing herself in the steady rhythm of another heartbeat joined with hers. She savored the feathery breath on her cheek, the strength of the loving embrace. For one, brief moment she was happy.

"Don't . . . forget," Gin-Yung cried.

"Never," the man answered huskily. His eyes opened wide, brown eyes, so deep and beautiful. "I love you, Gin-Yung . . . I'll always love you."

"Love . . . ," Gin-Yung breathed, the word vibrating around her. She felt arms around her, loving arms, guiding her . . . where? She was held close to a firmly beating heart, and she felt her breaths come in time with another's. Then the angel's lips found hers once more.

Cool waves of consciousness washed over

Gin-Yung, layer upon layer, building on itself. She felt her body go slack as she sank deeper and deeper into the watery depths, with no hope of resurfacing.

"That logic exam was a killer," Tom groaned under his breath. He and Danny had just handed in their blue exam books and were heading out the back door of the auditorium. "I don't think *any* of my answers were right."

"It wouldn't have been so bad if you had studied," Danny said, shrugging. He took the pair of sunglasses that had been tucked away in the front pocket of his pine green rugby shirt and slipped them on. "Don't mean to rub it in, but it was actually a pretty easy exam. He lifted every problem straight out of the textbook."

"Ugh! *Great*." Tom's nervous stomach churned. "Still, I could've memorized the entire book and it wouldn't have made any difference. I couldn't focus."

"Still worried about the letter, huh?"

Tom nodded solemnly and leaned against the back door until it opened. Since he put the letter in her in-box nearly twenty-two hours ago, Tom hadn't been able to think of anything else. Every muscle in his body was racked with tension, every nerve on edge, in anticipation of Elizabeth's answer. His happiness—his *future*—depended on it.

"The waiting is driving me crazy," Tom answered, his eyes downcast.

Danny gave his roommate a sympathetic pat on the shoulder. "Come on, Tombo—don't kill yourself over this. Elizabeth is an understanding person. If anyone can forgive a loser like you, she can."

Tom appreciated Danny's warped attempt at trying to make him feel better, but it only distressed him more. It was true that Elizabeth had an unusually forgiving nature. But even Elizabeth had her limits.

"I won't be able to rest until she gives me an answer," Tom remarked anxiously. The two of them wove in and out of the groups of students who were congregating outside the building to discuss the test. Tom unbuttoned the top button of his shirt and took a deep, uneasy breath.

Danny's brow furrowed in concern. "I'm not saying this is going to happen—because it's *not*—but let's say, for instance, that Elizabeth decides that she doesn't want to get back together with you. What are you going to do?"

"I don't know," Tom answered, a cold chill passing through him. "I'm afraid to find out."

They walked in silence around the back of the dining hall and crossed in front of the library. A few students were sitting on the stone steps reading while others gathered casually, stretching out on the green grass of the quad. Tom raised his eyes from the paved walkway and glanced over at the glass doors of the WSVU building. He broke out into a cold sweat. *Has Elizabeth stopped by since the last time I was there?* he wondered. *Has she seen the letter yet?*

"I have an idea," Danny said with the optimistic cheerfulness of a campus tour guide. "Why don't we drop by the snack bar and split a plate of atomic nachos? I guarantee that a double dose of jalapeños will get your mind off your love life . . . at least for a little while."

"Thanks, Wyatt. Maybe some other time." Tom's eyes were fixed on the station. "There's something I need to do."

Danny nodded slowly. "OK. But don't do anything crazy now, Wildman."

Before Danny even finished his sentence, Tom was jogging down the grassy slope toward the station. *If the envelope's gone, then at least I know she's read it,* Tom told himself, the pounding of his heart thundering in his ears. A film of sweat covered Tom's forehead as the station loomed nearer. His eyes were focused on the hypnotizing black-and-blue WSVU call letters stenciled on the glass doors.

Tom burst through the door of the station office like a marathon runner crossing the finish line. He leaned over and clutched his aching side while applause erupted from the corner of the room.

"Impressive show, Watts. You'll stop at nothing for a deadline."

Tom struggled to catch his breath and managed a polite smile. The joker was Scott Sinclair, a brand-new intern for the WSVU news staff. In the few days he'd been with WSVU, Scott had proven himself to be diligent, helpful, and good-natured, and Tom thought he made a great addition to the team.

"I'm glad you're here, Scott. We're way understaffed right now, and I'm never going to make the six o'clock broadcast at this rate. You can start by skimming through—"

"Oh, actually I'm not here to work," Scott interrupted. He was leaning against Elizabeth's desk with his arms crossed in front of him, one eyebrow cocked jauntily. "I'm looking for Elizabeth Wakefield. Have you seen her?"

Drawing himself to his full height, Tom was startled by Scott's bizarre change in attitude—from friendly to chilly. *What exactly is going on here?* he wondered. But his head was too busy with thoughts of Elizabeth to give Scott much attention. The most pressing matter was the letter.

Tom casually walked around to the side of Elizabeth's desk and looked it over. Everything was exactly as he had last seen it except for the in-box. The letter was gone.

Elizabeth took the letter. She took my letter.

A surge of panic pulsated from Tom's flushed cheeks down to his toes and back again. *She's got my letter,* he thought, his blood pressure rising. *Why isn't she here? Why isn't she waiting for me?* Tom shook his head slightly and tried to soothe his screaming nerves. *Maybe she hasn't read it yet. Maybe she took it with her and will open it later. Yes—that's what she must have done. Once she reads the letter, she'll come back.*

"So have you seen her?" Scott's voice was as clean and hard-edged as a stainless steel knife; it cut through Tom's frantic thoughts effectively.

"No," Tom answered, collapsing onto the couch. His weary body sank deep into the sagging cushions. *Don't freak out. Just be calm.* It wouldn't be long now before he had his answer. If he even got an answer. *No—don't think that way. You have to stay positive—*

"Do you know where she might be?" Scott pressed.

Tom eyed him strangely. "What do you want with her?"

"I just needed to talk to her about something, that's all," Scott answered impatiently. He stood up straight and put his hands in the pockets of his chinos. "Do you expect her back soon?"

"What?"

"Do you expect her back soon?"

As if I would tell you, Tom thought, thoroughly annoyed at Scott's arrogant stance. *Why does he need to see her?* Tom simply shrugged a response. He had too many other things on his mind.

"OK." Scott sighed as he began heading for the exit. "Forget I asked."

Jeez. That was weird, Tom thought, sinking back in the couch as soon as Scott had left. He closed his eyes and prayed for the queasy feeling in his gut to settle.

Do I expect her back soon? Tom wondered silently. *That's a very good question.*

Jessica tiptoed sheepishly into Nick's office, her face carefully hidden behind the enormous floral arrangement she was carrying. It was a peace offering of sorts, an apology for the temporarily-botched-but-ultimately-successful sting operation Jessica had wormed her way into the day before. She wasn't sorry in the least for her guest appearance—it was the most excitement she'd had without a charge card in *ages*— but she *did* regret upstaging Nick in front of his police buddies. She knew it would be a while before his fellow agents would let him live it down.

"Special delivery!" Jessica called in the sunniest voice she could muster as she carefully made her way toward Nick's desk. When she peered through two purple gladiolus stalks, Jessica spotted Nick hovering over some paperwork as if he didn't even hear her come in.

He's ignoring me, Jessica thought, slightly miffed. She dropped the flower vase unceremoniously in the middle of the papers Nick was reading. "I *said*, special delivery!"

Nick set down his pen and sniffed a drooping white lily, but his beautiful green eyes still didn't acknowledge Jessica's presence. Not one to be dismissed so easily, Jessica moved out from her floral camouflage and perched herself very visibly on the corner of Nick's desk.

"Are you still mad, sweetie?" Jessica asked, pouting her lower lip.

Nick's unshaven jaw tensed visibly. "That was a really stupid thing you did yesterday, Jess."

"I've never claimed to be a Frisbee champion," Jessica said. She crossed her legs seductively, hoping her hot black mini would melt Nick's icy stare. "And I've already told you I'd pay for the hubcap."

"I'm not talking about the hubcap," Nick snarled. The harshness of his tone was offset by the smoldering look that flickered in his eyes when he glanced at Jessica's tanned legs.

Now we're making some progress, Jessica thought, inching closer to him. "What did I do that was so stupid?"

Nick finally looked up at her. "You know

damn well what I'm talking about," he said irritably. "Going to the sting when I told you not to, almost wrecking an important case, nearly getting everyone on the team killed . . ."

"Almost and nearly don't count." Jessica snapped a peach rosebud off its stem and tucked the blossom behind her ear. "Everything turned out fine in the end, Nick. So why are you still mad at me?"

Sighing loudly, Nick looked up at her with tired eyes. "I'm not," he said, sounding like he was mad at himself for forgiving her. "You know I can't stay mad at you for long, Jess."

"Oh, good!" Jessica squealed, hopping off the desk and landing on Nick's lap. The jump sent his desk chair rolling back toward the wall. After they ricocheted off it, she threw her arms around Nick's neck and gave him a big, steamy kiss on the lips.

Nick smiled, making throaty sounds like a contented cat. "I don't know what it is about you, Jessica Wakefield, but you're under my skin." He tenderly brushed a strand of blond hair out of her eyes. "You're really something."

"No, you are, Nick!" Jessica blurted, bubbling over with enthusiasm. "The way you shot the gun out of that guy's hand! You were great! I had the best time watching you work! It was just so . . . so . . . exciting!"

"Well, thanks," Nick said with an embarrassed laugh. "I don't know what to say."

"Say we can do it again!" Jessica pressed the side of her face against his. "We were great together, Nick. Just like a team! Think of the criminals we could get off the streets. We'll be like Bonnie and Clyde!"

"Bonnie and Clyde were outlaws, Jess, not undercover cops."

Jessica rolled her eyes. "Whatever. You know what I mean." She gazed at him earnestly. The prospect of fighting crime with Nick filled her with a light, airy feeling, like she was being carried away by a hot-air balloon. "What do you say?"

Nick was suddenly silent. Deep lines furrowed his brow, and a vague, distant expression clouded his eyes. Jessica had never seen him look so preoccupied before; there was definitely something serious on his mind. All her excitement slowly trickled out of her. The hot-air balloon was in danger of a crash landing.

"Nick, what's the matter?" Jessica asked softly, dreading the answer. "Tell me. What's wrong?"

Chapter
Fourteen

"Nick, please talk to me—"

"Nothing," Nick lied. "Nothing's wrong." The truth was, while listening to Jessica rave about yesterday's sting, Nick was struck with a terrifying realization.

After the sting turned almost deadly for everyone involved, Nick had thought that Jessica would be sufficiently scared by it to finally give up her ridiculous quest for excitement. But nothing seemed to diffuse her desire. If anything, she wanted it even more than before.

The force of his realization hit him so hard, he could barely breathe. *I can't do this anymore,* he told himself. *There's no way I can stay on the force and be Jessica's boyfriend at the same time.*

"All we have to do is talk to Chief Wallace," Jessica chirped as if she hadn't noticed a single flicker of pain on Nick's face. She breezily hopped off Nick's lap and began pacing around the office.

When Jessica was on a roll, Nick knew there was no way of stopping her.

"I'm sure he'll be impressed with my performance yesterday. And I'll have to juggle my class schedule a bit, of course—especially if we get a case right away—but I don't mind missing a lecture or two if we're on call." Jessica stopped briefly to take a deep breath before resuming her hundred-mile-an-hour monologue. "Then there's the issue of a new wardrobe. As you saw yesterday, I have one acceptable sting outfit, but it's dry-clean only so I'll need at least six more, so that way I'll have every day of the week covered. Plus I'll need a new set for each season, naturally. I hope dry-cleaning bills are included in our expense account, because frankly I can't afford the cost of stain removal. You wouldn't believe how much they charge to get motor oil out of spandex. I found out the hard way. It's absolutely ludicrous—"

"Jess!" Nick shouted, his head whirling. "Take a breather for a minute."

Jessica ceased her rant and obediently collapsed into a chair.

"Let's think about this carefully," Nick urged, making one last appeal for her to change her mind. "You have the calendar shoot coming up soon, right?"

Jessica folded her arms impatiently in front of her. "Nick, I don't see what this has to do with anything."

"Think about it," he said slowly. "Let's say you and I go out on an assignment to bust some drug smugglers and one of them punches you in the face and gives you a black eye. What would you do?"

"I'd punch him right back!" Jessica shouted, thrusting her fist through the air.

Nick sighed and shook his head. "No . . . what I meant was, what would you do about the calendar shoot? If you get hurt, you're going to miss out on your dream of being a model. You could lose your chance of being in the calendar. You worked so hard for it."

Seemingly unswayed by Nick's argument, Jessica jumped to her feet. "Actually I've been thinking that a little undercover work would help me prepare for the shoot." Excitement gleamed in her eyes as she took off again. "I could pose for the calendar in a slinky police uniform, showing off some of the moves I've learned." Jessica lunged forward and raised her arms over her head like she was about to conk out an imaginary criminal with an imaginary wrench while pouting seductively the entire time. "Or I could be a kung fu heroine," she said, slicing the air with a roundhouse kick. "What do you think?"

Nick was too busy thinking about their future together to answer. He knew it was futile; there was no talking Jessica out of *anything*. More than anyone Nick understood the lure of excitement and danger of police work, and he could see the desire blazing in Jessica's naive eyes. Whatever his next assignment was, Nick was certain Jessica would follow him there too.

We were lucky yesterday, Nick thought solemnly, *but what about next time? Jessica could get hurt—or worse.* Nick remembered the terror that had gripped him during the sting. He never wanted to go through that torture again.

There was only one solution. *I'll have to stop seeing her,* he decided.

"Nick? What's wrong?" Jessica asked. "You have that look again."

Without saying a word Nick pulled Jessica close, holding her against his breaking heart. He didn't want it to be this way, but she left him no choice.

Jessica rested her head on Nick's shoulder, her soft blond hair grazing his cheek. "What's gotten into you? You're acting so weird."

Nick breathed in the warm, clean scent of Jessica's hair, afraid to let her go. *Don't make me choose between my job and being with you,* he pleaded silently. Jessica was the most incredible, beautiful, spirited woman he had ever met. There was no doubt in his mind that he loved Jessica with all his heart.

Nick pressed his cheek against hers and closed his eyes. *I love you so much, Jess,* Nick said silently. *The question is, do I love you enough to give up my career?*

A gray, misty rain fell on the green cemetery lawn while the trees swayed gently in the chilled morning air. Dressed in a black suit Todd sat in the last row of seats, eyelashes wet with tears and rain, his numb fingers holding a single, long-stemmed rose. The funeral service was ending, but Todd remained detached, refusing to look up at the opened casket.

"Todd, it's time," Elizabeth said, *touching him lightly on the arm. She stood up, along with her sister, Jessica, and the other Sweet Valley students who'd come. They each held white roses. Elizabeth nudged him again, but Todd didn't react. He only sat there silently, looking down at the rose he was holding.*

I miss you already, *Todd thought sadly as Gin-Yung's friends and loved ones filed out of their seats and approached the casket to say good-bye for the last time.*

220

An empty, hollow space had opened inside his chest, growing wider and deeper every minute that Todd was without her. It was sharp and cold, as if Todd had swallowed an iceberg, its jagged edges tearing at his broken heart.

Elizabeth and Jessica went ahead without him, solemnly joining the procession. A woman's cry rose up from across the gently rolling lawn. Todd lifted his face to the rain and saw the aggrieved looks on the faces of the entire Suh family, who were gathered under the tree.

Why did this have to happen to such a wonderful person? Todd asked silently, choking back a sob as he looked up at the sky. Why?

The line had almost reached the end, and everyone had carefully laid their roses inside Gin-Yung's casket. Everyone, that is, except Todd. He was the only person still seated, unable to move, unable to bid his girlfriend a final farewell.

Todd sat frozen. He felt as if his soul was a sky-scraper made of delicate threads of spun glass. The slightest movement or thought would shatter him to pieces.

Mr. Suh placed Todd's basketball jersey and a picture of the whole family inside the casket. After a final prayer Byung-Wah took the gleaming brass handle in both his hands and started to close the casket.

Todd bolted out of his seat, seized with a sudden

feeling of panic. He couldn't let her leave . . . not without saying good-bye.

"No—wait!" Todd called, tripping his way through the maze of chairs. Everyone turned and stared. Byung-Wah's arm froze in midair.

Todd fell to his knees beside the casket; cold, hard drops of rain pelted his face and mixed with his hot tears. A crushing pain seized his chest as his lungs struggled for air. Byung-Wah stepped aside while Todd grabbed for the handle and slowly re-opened the casket.

She was dressed in white. Draped in French lace, Gin-Yung lay serenely against the satin lining, her delicately folded hands resting on her rib cage. White rosebuds were scattered over her. Gin-Yung's beautiful face was tranquil, and her complexion was as fragile and colorless as a porcelain doll's.

She was the same Gin-Yung he had always known. All traces of her illness were gone.

"Oh, Gin-Yung . . ." A heavy, mournful sob rose from the depths of Todd's soul, choking him with sorrow. He gazed down at Gin-Yung's lovely, peaceful face in disbelief. *She can't be gone, he* thought as tears streaked down his cheeks. *She's too young to die. . . .*

Gently Todd laid his single, bloodred rose in Gin-Yung's casket, the long green stem carefully placed in her motionless hands. Then, leaning toward her, Todd tenderly touched his lips to

222

Gin-Yung's forehead, the whisper of his living breath meeting her eternal stillness. It was their last good-bye.

Elizabeth pressed her hand lightly on Todd's shoulder. "She's gone, Todd," she said thickly, helping him to his feet. "You have to let her go."

Todd squeezed his eyes shut, the pain of grief etching permanent scars on his heart. "It's all my fault!" he wailed. "I could've done something to save her!"

"There was nothing any of us could do," Elizabeth said gently, leading him away from the casket.

"I could have helped her get better. I could've helped her sooner. It's my fault she's dead!"

Byung-Wah reached for the brass handle and closed the casket, shutting Gin-Yung out of Todd's life forever.

"Nooo!" Todd broke free from Elizabeth's grasp and spread his arms across the casket and pressed his tearstained cheek against the glossy wooden lid. "I'm sorry I let you down, Gin-Yung," Todd sobbed bitterly as the cold rain poured down. "I'm so sorry. . . ."

"I'm so sorry . . . I'm so sorry," Todd muttered in his sleep, the sound of his own voice stirring him to consciousness. *It was only a dream,* Todd told himself as he struggled through the black void between sleep and wakefulness. The nightmare vanished, but the searing pain of grief in his chest lingered on.

Todd opened his weary eyes. When his vision cleared, he saw that he was stretched out on the empty hospital bed beside Gin-Yung's, apparently dozing off after a sleepless night. The room was filled with the fading light of late afternoon. No one else was around.

"I'm so glad you're still here," Todd whispered to Gin-Yung. She was completely still, almost seeming not to breathe, yet the steady beeps of her heart monitor reassured Todd that she was holding on.

Lying on his side, Todd propped his head on his hand and watched Gin-Yung's peaceful form. *There must be something I can do to make her well again. I can't just sit back and watch her go,* he thought with frustration. Ever since he was a small child, Todd had been taught that if he tried hard enough, he could accomplish anything he wanted—and so far it had held true in every aspect of his life.

But not this time.

This time nothing he did made Gin-Yung any healthier. Nothing he did gave Gin-Yung a hope for the future. Todd felt completely helpless. All he could do was sit and watch while she slipped away from him.

"I love you, Gin-Yung," Todd murmured, his

voice quivering and tearful. "I love you so much. I don't want to lose you." Never had he meant it so completely as he did at that very moment.

No matter what his reasons were for coming to visit Gin-Yung at first—friendship, obligation, pity, shock, respect, whatever—none of that mattered now, nor did Todd even remember it. All he knew was that during the last few days they'd spent together, Todd had fallen in love with her, more deeply and completely than he could remember or imagine. Her courage and dignity inspired him, and her pride stood strongly in the face of her older sister's claim that Gin-Yung's comfort and happiness were dependent on him.

In fact, Gin-Yung wasn't the dependent one. It was Todd who had become dependent on her, who had begun to live for her smile, the sparkle in her eyes, the gentleness of her touch. It was Todd who didn't think he could make it without her.

"Please, Gin-Yung," Todd whispered hoarsely. "Please don't leave me."

Suddenly the sounds in the room changed. Underneath all the other noises—whirring, humming, hissing—Todd realized that Gin-Yung's heart monitor had stopped beeping. The machine was emitting a constant, high-pitched whine.

Todd bolted upright and looked up at the dark green flat line on the machine. *I'm losing her,* Todd thought in panic as he dashed out into the hallway, looking for help. *I can't lose her. . . .*

"Somebody help me!" Todd shouted, his heart racing. "It's an emergency!"

Todd rushed back to Gin-Yung's bedside, hopeful that he had just been having a nightmare, but the monitor still showed a flat line.

Gasping breathlessly for air, Todd held Gin-Yung in his arms and touched her cold neck, searching for a pulse. "Hang on, Gin-Yung . . . you've got to hang on!"

The nurse ran into the room to see what the problem was. "I can't find her pulse!" Todd shrieked frantically. "Get the doctor!"

The nurse dashed off, and Mr. and Mrs. Suh came running in with the rest of the family behind them. Todd laid Gin-Yung back down on the bed and tried to perform CPR, praying he could revive her. The flat line screeched mercilessly in his ears.

"My child!" Mrs. Suh cried, throwing her arms around her daughter.

Mr. Suh held Chung-Hee against him. Tears rolled down their grief-stricken faces. "Ginny!" Chung-Hee screeched.

Todd gritted his teeth in despair. He breathed into Gin-Yung's mouth again with four quick, full breaths and listened for her to respond, but her lungs were silent.

Kim took his arm and tried to pull him away. "Todd—stop! Don't!"

"What more can I do?" Todd cried hysterically. *Don't go, Gin-Yung . . . please.* . . . With one hand on top of the other Todd desperately reached down and placed the heel of his hand just above her breastbone to begin cardiac massage.

But before Todd could go any further, Kim quietly put her arm around him, her eyes gently imploring him to stop. *It's over,* Kim seemed to be saying. *Let her go peacefully.*

Todd slowly dropped his arms at his sides. The flat line continued on, its pitch unrelenting. "Wait," Todd mumbled numbly as he backed away from the bed. His gaze shifted from Gin-Yung to Mr. Suh, then back to Kim, who was sobbing uncontrollably.

Finally he turned to Gin-Yung. She was there, and yet she wasn't.

Todd shook his head. "No," he said simply. "Oh, no."

The doctor rushed in and leaned over Gin-Yung to check her pulse. "I'm sorry," he said solemnly. "She's gone."

Staring in shock, Todd backed away involuntarily, back behind Gin-Yung's family. His heart was split wide open, leaving a terrifying chasm of pain and loneliness that stretched deeper and wider than he could have ever imagined. The air seemed to grow so hot and thick, it burned Todd's throat. The heavy weight on his chest pressed harder and harder; his lungs couldn't expand enough to breathe. *It can't be,* Todd thought, his stinging red eyes on the doctor as he gently dropped Gin-Yung's limp arm by her side. *She can't be . . .*

The doctor turned off the heart monitor and stepped back silently.

I can't take this—I have to get out of here. Todd struggled against the hot, oppressive atmosphere, his head reeling. *I can't stand another minute. . . .* Without saying a word he turned around and ran out the door.

Why did I have to leave my stupid portfolio at the station? Elizabeth asked herself irritably. She crossed the quad as quickly as her two-inch pumps would allow, fanning herself with her notebook so she wouldn't look completely melted and frazzled by the time she made it to the *Gazette* office. She knew that Scott and the senior editor were already waiting there for her, and she hoped her little slip of the brain wasn't going to make her too late for her interview.

Drops of perspiration beaded Elizabeth's brow—not from the hot, midday sun or the anxiety of the newspaper interview; not even from the possibility of running into Tom at the station. No, she was simply worried about what her own subconscious was trying to tell her.

She had meant to take the portfolio with her when she decided to try out for the *Gazette* the previous day, but it had completely slipped her mind. And now she had to head back there on a day when she was almost one hundred percent sure to run into Tom and was completely stressed out to boot. It was a telling sign that deeply disturbed her.

As she skipped down the slope toward the station she remembered an old adage her mother often said whenever they traveled: *If you accidentally leave something behind, it means that you never wanted to go.*

Elizabeth's cheeks burned hot. *Could it be true?* she wondered. *Is my subconscious trying to tell me something, or was it just a simple case of forgetfulness?*

Just as Elizabeth was nearing the intimidating glass doors of the station, she caught sight of something that made her heart stop. It was Todd.

Red-faced, he was staggering toward her, clutching at his side as if he had been running for miles. Elizabeth froze in place. As Todd moved closer, Elizabeth could see that he had been crying.

Oh no. Gin-Yung . . . The notebook slipped

out of Elizabeth's hand and fell to the ground. One look at the pained expression on his face and Elizabeth felt a cold chill run through her body. Todd didn't have to tell her anything— she already knew.

"Oh, Todd," Elizabeth murmured, taking him into her arms. She gasped from the force and urgency of Todd's embrace. He clutched her desperately, as if he were holding on for dear life, and buried his damp face in her neck.

"She's gone. . . ." Todd's voice was cracked and hollow. After drawing in a deep, quivering breath Todd suddenly let all his pain out, his body shaking with wrenching sobs. He cried with all his strength, tears of sorrow pouring freely from his tormented brown eyes.

Elizabeth tenderly stroked Todd's head, tears stinging her own eyes. His grief seemed to pass right through her with each stabbing breath.

"I'm so sorry, Todd," Elizabeth whispered, holding Todd as tightly as she could. "I'm so sorry she's gone."

"She's coming . . . she's coming . . ." Tom sang the words ecstatically as he drummed his hands on the side of his desk.

Only a few seconds ago he had been unsuccessfully working on some copy and trying to ignore the gnawing sensation in his stomach, when he glanced out the window and saw Elizabeth running—almost *skipping*—up the path. She was looking radiant and gorgeous, as usual. But today she'd put on the floral dress Tom loved so much.

She read the letter! he told himself, his heart bounding joyously in his chest. *She read the letter, and she's coming to forgive me!*

Tom scuffled about the station, trying to find something to do so he wouldn't look like he was waiting for her. He smoothed back his hair and tucked in his blue dress shirt, imagining how Elizabeth would throw her arms around him passionately and kiss him with her sweet lips. *Tonight we're going to celebrate,* Tom thought excitedly. He wanted to take her to the best restaurant in town. He wanted to take her dancing on the beach in the moonlight. Anything she wanted. He vowed to make this night the best night of her life.

Several long minutes passed while Tom shuffled papers at his desk and drank from his mug of coffee, trying to look casual. "Where is she?" he muttered expectantly under his breath. Elizabeth had only been a few steps away from the station when he saw her—she should've come inside by now.

Tom returned to his papers, his excited feet tapping impatiently against the floor. *What if she turned around?* whispered a little voice inside his head. *What if she changed her mind?*

Tom bounded out of his chair, coffee cup still in hand, and ran to the door. *I'm not going to let you walk away, Elizabeth, not after coming this far,* he promised silently. *I'm not going to lose you again.* Tom raced out into the hallway and headed toward the glass doors, pacing and sipping from his coffee mug, trying not to look as though he was desperately waiting for her return.

That's when he saw her.

Elizabeth hadn't turned around after all. She was standing in front of the station locked in a fiery embrace with Todd Wilkins.

No . . . Tom's blood ran cold as he watched them rock back and forth together with Todd's face buried in Elizabeth's neck and her hands stroking his back. They were obviously in love.

There's your answer, Watts. Elizabeth had read the letter, all right, and she was flinging Tom's apology right back in his face. It was an act of pure, defiant revenge.

So that's how it's going to be, Tom challenged silently, pressing his palm flat against the hard glass. Rage boiled inside him as he watched Elizabeth's shameless embrace. She had ruthlessly aimed for Tom's heart, and she had hit her mark with merciless success.

I was a fool for ever thinking we could be

together again. Elizabeth and I are over. Forever.
Tom raised his coffee mug and hurled it with explosive fury against the wall, watching it shatter into thousands of pieces.

Bruce Patman has been fatally poisoned . . . but he still has a few hours left to live! With the help of Lila Fowler and Jessica Wakefield, can he discover who wants him dead—and why—before it's too late? Find out in the next Sweet Valley University Thriller Edition, DEAD BEFORE DAWN.

SIGN UP FOR THE SWEET VALLEY HIGH® FAN CLUB!

Hey, girls! Get all the gossip on Sweet Valley High's® most popular teenagers when you join our fantastic Fan Club! As a member, you'll get all of this really cool stuff:

- Membership Card with your own personal Fan Club ID number
- A Sweet Valley High® Secret Treasure Box
- Sweet Valley High® Stationery
- Official Fan Club Pencil (for secret note writing!)
- Three Bookmarks
- A "Members Only" Door Hanger
- Two Skeins of J. & P. Coats® Embroidery Floss with flower barrette instruction leaflet
- Two editions of *The Oracle* newsletter
- Plus exclusive Sweet Valley High® product offers, special savings, contests, and much more!

Be the first to find out what Jessica & Elizabeth Wakefield are up to by joining the Sweet Valley High® Fan Club for the one-year membership fee of only $6.25 each for U.S. residents, $8.25 for Canadian residents (U.S. currency). Includes shipping & handling.

Send a check or money order (do not send cash) made payable to "Sweet Valley High® Fan Club" along with this form to:

SWEET VALLEY HIGH® FAN CLUB, BOX 3919-B, SCHAUMBURG, IL 60168-3919

NAME _____
(Please print clearly)

ADDRESS _____

CITY_____ STATE _____ ZIP_____
(Required)

AGE_____ BIRTHDAY_____ /_____ /_____

Offer good while supplies last. Allow 6-8 weeks after check clearance for delivery. Addresses without ZIP codes cannot be honored. Offer good in USA & Canada only. Void where prohibited by law.
©1993 by Francine Pascal   LCI-1383-123